EL NINO
THE MYSTERY OF THE GOLD
STATUE OF THE CHRIST CHILD

EL NINO
THE MYSTERY OF THE GOLD STATUE OF THE CHRIST CHILD

A Novel

By

Ferrel Glade Roundy

About the Book

This is the story of the famed gold statue of **El Nino**, the Christ Child, that up until about 1920 graces the Cathedral of the Blessed Virgin in Ascension, Northern Mexico. Pilgrims come from near and far to be healed of their physical and spiritual maladies by looking into the eyes of this remarkably life-like statue, which was crafted from 50 lbs. of pure gold by famed sculptor Luigi Arturo of Florence, Italy. Pancho Villa and his men try desperately to abscond with **El Nino**, but their efforts are thwarted by silver-tongued Padre Silvaro de Escalante. So to avoid further run-ins with Villa, the padre and associates at the cathedral pack the famed statue in clay so it can be transported secretly up over the U.S. border to a sacred cave just north of Camarra, a small town in New Mexico next to the Arizona border. But conditions there force them to continue north and cross over into Arizona, then into Utah's spectacular Monument Valley just west of Four Corners; finally, after crossing the Colorado River, they arrive at Grand Bench, the extreme southeastern side of the Kaiparowits Plateau [now encompassed by the Grand Staircase-Escalante National Monument]. There a cave is manifested to them as the temporary hiding place of **El Nino** until the political agitation in Northern Mexico subsides. This harrowing journey is fraught with hair-raising encounters. Eventually rumor with her thousand tongues spreads word that a treasure, allegedly a gold statue of Jesus, is concealed in one of the caves on Grand Bench. Treasure seekers, some heavily armed, converge upon this area. Two men from the town of Escalante actually discover the statue but soon find it to be a slippery commodity. Ferrel Glade Roundy's intriguing novel **EL NINO** reveals what happens to this famed gold statue of the Christ Child. Definitely a **must** read!

ASCENSION

"Bring ye your rings, earrings, bracelets, necklaces, brooches, decorative chains, and all other golden paraphernalia at your disposal," they had been asked, "that we may melt them down and thus create the transcendently beautiful and sacred statue of El Nino, the Christ Child, for He shall have healing in His wings!"

Thus admonished was an entire generation of the faithful living within the environs of Ascension and throughout that general region. They came to the Cathedral of the Blessed Virgin with its white marble statue of the Virgin Mother to unburden themselves of their personal treasures, be these large or small or barely the equivalent of the Widow's mite. Every faithful soul who could contribute did, and in time the famed sculptor Luigi Arturo of Florence, Italy, was summoned to journey across the sea to Mexico to work his magic with their gold.

Excitement grew when the news of his arrival was noised about by word of mouth throughout the region. Speculation was rampant as to the exact dimensions El Nino would take.

"How will Senor Arturo know what El Nino should look like?" asked Senora Cecilia de Amador, who had given generously of her family's personal treasure.

"I have it on unimpeachable authority," said Padre Silvaro de Escalante, "that this renowned artist, Signor Arturo, is reputed to commune with God when conceptualizing the countenance of what is to be a sacred statue. Thus I can assure you, Hermana de Amador, that your generous offerings in support of this worthy project will turn into wellsprings of happiness to fill your soul forever."

"Padre de Escalante," the gracious lady smilingly responded, "with such words as these I will wait until the rapturous moment when the statue of El Nino will be finished and revealed for the first time to the large throng of believers."

The arrival of Signor Arturo sparked a day-long celebration with everyone waiting to shake his hand and wish him Godspeed in his noble endeavor.

"When will you begin, Senor Arturo?" a little boy asked.

"Tomorrow morning bright and early, my son," the famed sculptor said. "Yes, bright and early 'manana,' I believe you say in Spanish."

The news spread, and the entire city along with all of the smaller towns nearby rejoiced, everyone placing great faith in the renowned sculptor with such gifted hands, for word had it that El Nino would be endowed somehow with wondrous healing powers.

"Padre de Escalante," three little girls said as they tugged at his robe to get his attention while he was conversing with a group of adults, "grandmother has entrusted us with these precious golden earrings, pure gold they are. Said she, 'Give these to our good padre and tell him they are to be melted down to become a part of El Nino.' So here they are, padre."

"Oh, bless you, my little ones," the tall and handsome padre said smiling. "Say muchas gracias to Senora Isabella, your wonderful grandmother. Tell her El Nino will smile sweetly on her, for she has contributed generously and often to this blessed cause."

And thus it went with additional offerings pouring in, the givers wanting desperately to be counted among those on whom El Nino, as promised, would smile while extending His blessings for their undaunted faithfulness. . . .

Using plaster of paris, Signor Arturo worked unceasingly till he had fashioned the face and figure that would become El Nino. But, of course, Padre de Escalante and a select few were the only ones privileged to see the plaster of paris production. All were overawed by the benign and loving countenance of the lifelike statue.

"Surely this good man Senor Arturo must truly be inspired," Padre Ernesto exclaimed. "No mortal in and of himself could conceive such a countenance. Why, it is so lifelike that I'd not be surprised if the statue spoke to us."

"All true," Padre de Escalante replied. "How very fortunate we are to have Signor Arturo as our sculptor. Perhaps the very Mother of God has been guiding his talented hands. After all, the

Holy Virgin would have a vested interest in any replica of her blessed Son, would she not? . . ."

Work proceeded without delay, and in due time while the general excitement was running high, the statue of El Nino received the finishing touches. Then in a special convocation for the faithful, several thousand souls---men, women, and children---were privileged to take their first glimpse of El Nino. This magnificent creation, everyone agreed, had resulted from especially inspired hands.

"Might those skilled hands actually have been the hands of God?" asked Senor Camacho, the large landowner who provided employment for almost a hundred men and women. . . ."Elisa," Senora Bustillos whispered to her daughter as they stopped to view the already famous statue, "I feel so strange. It is as if this statue, this consummate work of gold, were actually alive. Look closely, my dear, and you will feel His eyes following you, indeed peering into your very soul."

"I have looked, mother," Elisa replied half under her breath, "and I am afraid to look again for fear El Nino may even speak to me. Standing before Him I no longer have any secrets at all---He knows them. I swear He does. I can feel it."

"And I," her mother added, "perceive a special warmth emanating from El Nino. No longer do I feel bilious, and my arthritic pains are no more! I have just witnessed a miracle in myself! Indeed I have. . . ."

"Bring your little ones," Padre de Escalante had requested, "for of such is the kingdom of heaven---so said the Lord Himself. Yea, let them come unto me, and forbid them not."

And they had come, many being carried, for they were crippled. But no one has more faith than a little child, and many little crippled children carried in to see the statue of El Nino for the first time, suddenly exclaimed, "I can walk! I just know it! I can walk! Oh, please put me down so I can walk!"

And they did walk! Then amidst tears of joy a great hush came over the multitude as if they were in the very presence of God. Darkness gradually descended upon the city, but the faithful along with occasional skeptics or curiosity seekers kept coming. When they exited the cathedral, however, they suddenly

3

had become believers. El Nino had gazed into their souls, and they knew it. Their shades of doubt had dissipated like dew in the morning sun. Additional candles, they assumed, had to be lit not for ceremonial purposes but rather to provide light to combat the approaching darkness. Then another miracle occurred for believers and nonbelievers alike to see. El Nino was illuminating the darkness. A radiance like no earthly light that anyone had ever seen was emanating from the statue. Those passing by were touched, moved upon, as never before, their whole being aware of the warmth of love flowing from El Nino to them.

Outside the cathedral hundreds were congregated where, faces tear-stained and voices hushed, they were discussing their miraculous healings. In the distance one man, a known congenital cripple, was running and leaping and shouting for joy. "I am healed!" he exclaimed again and again. "El Nino has healed me! El Nino hath made me whole! Only minutes ago I was but half a man, the mere shell of a man, but look at me now! I can run and not be weary! I can walk and not faint! Praise be to God, for His Son as manifested through El Nino hath taken away my wretched infirmities and buried them in the depths forever!"

A mother, who of necessity had always carried her little epileptic daughter, cried out enraptured, "Praise God! She is healed! Look at her, my friends and neighbors. This child who couldn't walk and who was subjected to periodic fits and body-wracking muscle spasms, is running and leaping like a jumping jack. She'll not even sleep tonight, nor will I, so great is our joy!"

Then a woman known to have thrown herself into the fire, her body covered with scars, cried out, "O blessed Jesus, praise be unto Thee, for Thou has cast out the foul spirits that forced me to do the most horrendous things to myself. But now I am FREE! I AM MYSELF ONCE AGAIN! Life is glorious beyond my poor power to say. All I know is that El Nino hath made me whole, and I shall praise God forever! . . ."

And thus passed this day the likes of which no one in that vast throng had ever witnessed or even dreamed possible. More such days followed as word spread far and wide about the beneficent results of merely standing in the presence of El Nino.

The "El Nino Effect," as it came to be called, was commensurate with an individual's faith---the greater one's faith, the greater the blessing emanating from the statue. In time all visitors began to remove their shoes as they drew near to the Cathedral of the Blessed Virgin, for as someone said, "The ground whereon ye stand is holy ground." Thus, like Moses before the burning bush, they removed their shoes before coming into view of El Nino.

But, of course, to those adulterated in spirit, El Nino was nothing more than a fifty-pound statue of pure gold that, melted down, would make the bearer thereof independently wealthy. Along with the great outpouring of faith and the steadily increasing number of healings, more and more untoward comments began filtering through to Padre de Escalante, who commented philosophically that "there must needs be opposition in all things."

"Ernesto," the padre was moved to say to his assistant, who was like faithful Achates to Aeneas,"I perceive the time to be ripe for us to undertake the little excavation job we were discussing recently."

"I'm of the same opinion, Silvaro," Ernesto said. "When do we begin?"

"Tomorrow. I've studied the plans, and they appear to be foolproof. We've been too greatly blessed to let our beloved El Nino fall prey to any charlatans that might have designs upon it, and it is eminently clear that such are gathering for the coming storm."

Early next morning a special and highly secret excavation project commenced in a basement room directly underneath El Nino. Within two weeks a hole some six feet across and roughly a hundred feet deep had been dug. The plan was to go about twenty-five feet deeper, but to their amazement the workers struck water and had to cease digging. Reporting this to Padre de Escalante, they apologized for their inability to cope with nature.

"What you've done is splendid," the friendly padre assured them, winking at their leader. "The presence of water is actually a boon to us!"

During the excavation skilled artisans had been busy constructing a highly sophisticated trapdoor in front of the statue.

It was so well concealed that none but the trained eye could perceive, and none but Sanchez, the cathedral's caretaker, was permitted to enter the room directly beneath El Nino.

"Let us pray, Ernesto," Padre de Escalante said to his trusted friend in the faith, "that conditions never deteriorate to the point where this special contingency plan has to be made operative. But if the need arises, we'll have this at our disposal."

"Indeed, Silvaro," Padre Ernesto stated, "but war clouds again are louring upon the horizon. You no doubt have heard that just days ago some of Pancho Villa's men actually crossed over the U. S. border and raided the little community of Columbus, New Mexico, where they shot a number of people, looted several business, and otherwise ransacked the place, leaving our Yankee neighbors stunned, baffled, outraged, and primed for revenge."

"Yes, my friend," de Escalante said, showing a look of concern. "I also have heard that this Villa, self-styled general he perceives himself to be, is well aware of El Nino and the statue's great commercial value. . . ."

PANCHO VILLA

Northern Mexico's state of Chihuahua is a desolate and windblown country with vast open spaces stretching uninvitingly between the inaccessible Sierras dotted with scattered haciendas, mines, and settlements. The whole area had proven ideal for guerrilla warfare. From time to time various groups of desperados came swooping down from the mountains on horseback to raid isolated federal garrisons and steal horses, provisions, guns, and ammunition, plus raiding ranches and mining camps. They were particularly adept at riding suddenly into small towns and taking over for a while, brutally torturing and even killing those who resisted them. They also had sharp eyes for attractive women and younger girls, many of whom they raped repeatedly and otherwise mistreated. Their actions bore many similarities to those of the Norsemen who for several centuries plagued the West Coast of Europe and later Britain before finally settling down to intermarry with the local citizens. These Mexican hell-raisers or revolutionaries---call them what you will---were equally akin to the Asiatic hordes that came sweeping into one unsuspecting settlement after another, looting, ransacking, raping, and killing.

The Mexican revolution attracted not only aggrieved and disenfranchized citizens but also the criminal element such as the cattle thief and murderer Dorotea Arango, popularly known by his assumed name: **Pancho Villa**. Though purportedly illiterate, Villa displayed natural leadership and an uncanny talent for maneuvering over vast areas. Able to make intelligent decisions while in the saddle, he seemed possessed of a surprising knowledge of friend and foe alike. Moreover, he exuded a charisma that drew those of his ilk to him.

Cruel, anarchistic, and part Indian, Villa was a tough hombre to deal with on his own turf. For a number of months he and his followers rampaged, literally raising hell and for a time paralyzing the entire economy of Chihuahua. Trains even stopped running or were in the hands of rebels, who in addition occupied haciendas, towns, and mines. Depredations of the worst kind were heaped upon the citizenry, and Mexico's usually corrupt government seemed powerless to intervene effectively.

That Pancho Villa would get wind of El Nino in the little town of Ascension was a given. His mouth was said to water when he first heard of the famed gold statue that purportedly weighed some fifty pounds.

"Did you hear that, men!" Villa exclaimed. "**Fifty** pounds of pure gold! Madre de Dios, I must look into this pronto. But first, Gustavo, I'd like you to take eight or ten men and visit the cathedral in Ascension. If memory serves me correctly, it is called the Cathedral of the Blessed Virgin. Go there as humble suppliants interested in seeing El Nino and perhaps even confessing your sins, which are many!" he said, bursting out in uproarious laughter. "Would that I could be there as a little mouse, Gustavo, to see you and Raul confessing your sins. You'd keep the poor padre up all day and night listening to your litany of wrongdoings! In fact, I'm not so sure you could list all of them in a day and a night. You'd probably require an entire week! In any case, go there ostensibly to confess your sins, but return with the statue if you can."

SINNERS MEET SAINTS

The sun's first rays next morning shone on Villa's chief lieutenant, Gustavo Marcas, and eight hand-picked men as they rode north over the dreary wasteland between their hideout and the peaceful little town of Ascension. Word of their arrrival spread fast, with shops and businesses pulling the shutters and shades and putting metal grates in place to protect themselves from the onslaught.

Mothers were quick to hide their daughters from the marauders, for the latter always seemed to be endowed with an overabundance of testosterone and an almost total lack of humanity and decency. The crimes committed by this breed of men were legion, and law-abiding citizens naturally were wary each time a group of strange and unfamiliar horsemen came riding into their community. More often than not, such men were up to no good. This time was no different.

Approaching the cathedral, they were discussing how they could make off with a fifty-pound gold statue. In a lighter vein Raul said, "Gustavo, is it true that you, too, plan to confess your sins before we depart from the cathedral with our loot?"

"I wouldn't miss the chance for anything," the feisty lieutenant said laughing. "But if I confess, then you likewise must confess, Raul. And then if fate should decree that either one or both of us should be forced to meet our Maker before the time, we at least can meet Him with a clear conscience!"

Inside, the priests, alerted to the men's approach, had told the few worshipers to leave quickly by the back door. Outside, Gustavo said, "Francisco and Juan, go in and have a look around the joint; then report back to me. If you've not returned in ten minutes, we'll come looking for you."

Entering the cathedral, they were met by Padre de Escalante walking toward them. "Good afternoon, gentlemen. Peace be with you," he said smiling, revealing a mouthful of pearly white teeth.

"Good afternoon, Padre," both men said in unison while instinctively removing their hats.

"Do you come in peace, gentlemen?" Padre de Escalante queried.

"By all means, Padre," Francisco said. "Our work as of late has not permitted us to confess our sins, and for this reason we have come. But first we are most interested in having a close-up look at the famed statue of El Nino. By the way, Padre, you appear to be alone this afternoon. Is this the usual siesta time here in Ascension?"

"Yes, I'm afraid so. Worshipers usually begin to trickle in at about two o'clock, and within an hour the pews are filled. Many of the worshipers are afflicted with a multitude of physical, mental, and spiritual maladies. Many of the pitiful souls who come here to pray and meditate and, in effect, to commune with El Nino usually end up healed or otherwise relieved of their afflictions. For this reason people come from great distances, some of late even coming from foreign lands and at considerable expense and sacrifice to experience the healing powers of El Nino, which statue of course is merely symbolical of the Christ."

"Some statue I should say," Juan commented. "Do you think, Padre, that if I exercised faith I, too, could be cured of my negative tendencies?" And when he winked at Francisco, both of them burst out laughing.

Unruffled by their insolence, Padre de Escalante said, "Gentlemen, I perceive that you do come in peace, but one thing disturbs me."

"And what might that be, Padre?" Francisco said sarcastically.

"If you truly have come in peace, gentlemen, then why did you not remove your weapons before entering this house of the Lord? God, you know, is a God of peace and love. Is it truly peace and the love of God, my friends, that bring you here today?"

"Well, Padre," Francisco said, "part of what you've said brings us here today: love. But not the love of God. 'Tis the love of money, the love of pure gold, that brings us here. And if I might speak candidly, that gold statue right up there is why we've come. When we leave this building, that statue goes with us. Got that, Padre?" And with these brazen words both men again laughed.

Still calm, Padre de Escalante smiled and said, "I understand, gentlemen. In this case, let me show you the statue. Follow me, please."

"Not so fast there, Padre," Juan said, pulling a pistol from its holster and pointing the weapon at the padre. "**Now** you may lead us to the statue; and though we hate to do it, Padre, circumstances force us to tie you up and to stick a big piece of that robe in your mouth so you can't call out for help."

"Oh, that goes without saying, gentlemen," Padre de Escalante said quite jovially. "In fact, I'd be taken aback if you should overlook such an obvious amenity. Indeed, I'd say that you were just a couple of bumblers, rank beginners. But in looking into your eyes, I see that you are practiced criminals, not mere beginners." The padre said this as he was leading the men up to the statue of El Nino. Then standing directly in front of the statue, he said, "Do you notice, gentlemen, that El Nino's face, usually benign and full of love, is displeased with you and your unkind attitude?"

"Look, Padre," Francisco said, his voice tipped with anger, "that you're wearing that black robe doesn't mean nothin to us. And we'd advise you to watch your tongue."

Undisturbed at this outburst, Padre de Escalante again smiled. "My goodness, do I shiver and shake in my boots now or tomorrow? Which time would you recommend?"

Francisco's face white with anger, he suddenly doubled up his right fist and swung at the padre, who dodged the blow and clipped Francisco squarely on the chin, fairly lifting him off his feet and landing him on the back of his head, whose thud along with that of the falling pistol echoed throughout the building.

"Why, you son of a . . ."

"Tut, tut," the padre said to Juan, "don't forget where you are. This is is the Lord's house, and He doesn't countenance profanity in here."

"Listen then, you brazen bastard," Juan said as Francisco, finally gathering his wits about him, staggered to his feet while rubbing his chin, "I ought to fill you full of lead right here and now."

"But why would you want to do such a thing prematurely?" Padre de Escalante asked. "After all, I'm your guide, and out of the goodness of my big heart, I must explain how this magnificent statue can be removed from its resting place. You see, unless I reveal the key to you gentlemen, you would not be able to remove the statue. And somehow I get the distinct impression that you are hellbent on removing it. Now, Senor," he said to Francisco, "if you will be so kind to step right here directly in front of the statue and place your left arm on the left side and your right arm on the right side and see if you can create a slight rocking motion from side to side, the supports holding the statue in place will release and, voila! the statue will be yours merely for the asking. Isn't it embarrassingly simple? And to think that you absolutely could not have removed it without this bit of expert advice."

The two desperados glanced at one another as if to ask if the padre was for real. "Go ahead, Francisco," Juan said. "I've got this wise guy here covered and won't hesitate to plug him right between the horns if he tries anything."

Thus encouraged, Francisco stepped forward and extended both hands to touch the statue. Just as they made contact with the base of El Nino, a trapdoor suddenly opened and Francisco dropped out of sight, to be seen no more. And at that very instant Padre Ernesto, stepping from behind a curtain, shoved Juan into the opening. First a scream was heard and then a second later a mighty splash, followed by another scream and a dull thud, indicating that Juan had landed ungently on top of his partner in mischief.

Looking at Ernesto and grinning, Padre de Escalante called down through the opened trapdoor, "Sanchez, please close the trapdoor securely and then open two sacks of lime and empty their contents into the abys."

"I already have them opened and ready, Padre," a voice from down below replied.

"Good man, Sanchez. Please remain at your post, for it is likely that we'll have more business."

Padre Ernesto, grinning, stepped back behind the curtain as Padre de Escalante proceeded to walk down the aisle in anticipation of the next entrants. Quickly he picked up Francisco's fallen pistol and secured it under his robe. Almost like clockwork the cathedral door opened and two more gunmen entered, their spurs jingling as they walked toward the padre.

"Welcome, gentlemen, and a pleasant afternoon to you," the padre said smiling. "To what do I owe this singular honor? 'Tis not often that gun-toting parishioners enter the house of the Lord. Is this a new fashion you're introducing? Or do you conduct yourself in this manner elsewhere?"

Taken aback by the apparent friendliness and strange questioning, the two men at first didn't know how to respond. Then the one, gathering his wits about him, said, "Padre, two of our friends came in here about ten minutes ago. What happened to them? Where'd they go anyway?"

"Oh, those two men!" the padre said lightheartedly. "Noting how windblown and thirsty they appeared, we invited them downstairs for a repast of shewbread and cool red wine. As to be expected, they unhesitatingly accepted our gracious offer. And just now I was on my way outside to invite the rest of you gentlemen to come in and have a drink on the house. It's an old custom here in the Cathedral of the Blessed Virgin. In fact, we initiated this custom at about the same time that we installed this fifty-pound statue of El Nino---all pure gold, you know. Naturally before you go downstairs for a drink you'll want to follow me up front to have a close-up look at El Nino. I must ask, however, if you gentlemen have come in a spirit of peace or if you perchance might be inspired by ulterior motives of one kind or another. Which is it, gentlemen?"

Suspicious and impatient by this time, Carlos Huberto said, "All right, Padre, cut the crap."

"Oh my," the padre said, assuming a pained expression, "what an unbecoming word to utter in the Lord's house! You **have** come with ill intent. I can see it. Yes, let me read your thoughts. Indeed, my intuition tells me that, impervious to the remarkable beauty and healing powers of this statue, you intend to ride off into the sunset with it and melt it down merely for the money. Am I right?"

"Yes, Padre," Carlos said, his patience wearing thin. "You're right. We do intend to ride off with this statue, and neither you nor anyone else is going to stop us. Understand?"

"Perfectly. I understand perfectly," the padre countered. "Why, how could I **not** understand? Men with the sterling character of you gentlemen, having thought out your future plans well, are always decisive in determining what they want to do. By the way, will you gentlemen share this gold with others or hog it all unto yourselves? Surely you wouldn't have it in you to be selfish, would you? After all, wouldn't it be utterly disgraceful if the time ever came when thieves couldn't trust one another!"

"Look, Padre," Carlos said, "if you don't cut the bullshit right now, we're going to cut off a big piece of your fancy robe and stuff it down your thoat."

"Oh, heavens, gentlemen, don't do a thing like that. You see, I gag easily and would not want to make a mess here in the cathedral. . . . Okay, enough said. Simply follow me up to the statue so I can explain how to release it from its base. Otherwise, try as you might, you would not be able to make off with the fifty pounds of pure gold."

Both men, shaking their heads in disbelief at such a bizarre reception, followed the padre up to the statue. "Now, gentlemen," the padre said, "may I ask you to look directly into the face of El Nino? Good. Now tell me something truthfully. Do your eyes not water when you look into the face of this statue? Oh, I see that they do? And do you not feel a strange heat coming from the statue? You do? And does it not cause a burning sensation in your innards? It does. Could it be, gentlemen, that your hearts are not pure? And since this statue of El Nino actually represents the Christ, do you realize that with unrepentant eyes you, in effect, have just looked upon the face of the Savior?"

Suddenly turning to his bemused partner, Carlos, hands shaking noticeably, said, "Roberto, I don't know about you, but forget this damned statue. I'm gittin outa here right now. If any

14

of the others want to come in here and confront this weird padre and his equally weird statue, that's their business. I want no part of it. Do you feel the heat coming from this thing?"

"That I do, Carlos. I'm with you. Let's git outa here pronto!"

Both men lost no time exiting the building. Outside, both of them appeared shaken and distraught. "Look, Gustavo," they exclaimed almost in unison, "you can go in there if you want, but we've just had an experience that neither one of us wants to repeat."

"All right, you two sissified jackasses," Gustavo said, displaying a bit of bravado to impress his men, "what in the hell's goin on in there anyway? We've been waitin out here for at least twenty minutes. Four men go in, but only two return. Where's the other two?"

"We don't know. The padre said they'd gone downstairs to eat and drink. That's all we know. He invited us to do the same ---after we had gazed upon the statue at close range. He even volunteered to tell us how to disconnect the statue from its mount, but he showered us with so much bullshit in the meantime that we got antsy about the whole affair, and that's why we're here. Why don't **you** go in, Gustavo? You're not afraid of God, man, or devil. Let's see you and one or two of these other fellers go in. We'll be waitin anxiously for your return to hear what you think of the experience."

"I swear," Gustavo said, "that in all my born days I've never encountered a situation quite like this one. We came here to steal that statue. We send four men in to survey the joint and, if possible, to come walking out with fifty pounds of gold. You came walking out all right, but where amidst hell's bells is that damned statue? And where have them other numbskulls gone?"

The rest of the banditos, now nervous and fidgety, looked at one another. "Men," Gustavo said, "if we're not back out here in, say, ten minutes, come in after us; and if you have to come in with guns blazing, then do so. We've come here to remove that fifty-pound gold statue, **pure** gold I'm told, from this building; and, come hell or high water, we're gonna do it. Mark my word. Now, Ramon and Gilberto, come with me."

Just then a little group of about six or eight worshipers, among them two small girls being carried on stretchers, had approached the cathedral unnoticed and were about to enter. "You there!" Gustavo bellered. "Git away from that door! I don't want you goin in there. Now git the hell outa here. Go back to where you came from, and do it pronto!"

"But, Senor," remonstrated the mother of the two pitiful little girls being carried, "we've come a long way so that my little daughters could look upon El Nino and be healed!"

"So they can be WHAT? HEALED did you say? Are you outa your mind? How in the hell do you propose to go in there and be healed by looking at a dumb statue?"

"Senor, I can't tell you how it happens. I can only tell you that it does, for I have seen it with my own eyes. My sister's husband, who had not walked in seven years, came here and . . ."

"Bullshit! Now git the hell outa here right now before me and my men give you some unwanted assistance." Noting the hurt and disappointed looks among this pathetic little group, Gustavo began to weaken in his resolve, but only for an instant, for he wanted to make himself look good in the eyes of Pancho Villa, who would sing and dance and shout merrily at seeing fifty pounds of pure gold. "Now git outa here this instant, and don't let me have to tell you again," he said in his sternest tones.

Slowly and without real resolve, the little group turned around and started moving away from the cathedral steps. Gustavo and his two partners glanced briefly at the rest of their heavily armed minions of mischief, who had moved several feet to one side to enjoy the shade of a large tree. "Now, men," the feisty lieutenant told them, "if we're not back out here in ten or twelve minutes, the rest of you are to bust into the joint. When we leave here, it will be with fifty pounds of pure gold, and that's that!"

Inside, Amado Garcia, an altar boy standing on an upper level of the cathedral and looking out, said, "Padre de Escalante, three tough-looking hombres are comin in."

"Gracias, Amado. Remember now what I've taught you about using those pistols, and don't get rattled. Use 'em if you have to, but make sure you have to, son." Then calling out to his

16

assistant he said, "Ernesto, stay outa sight, but keep a sharp eye out for trouble. This rabble seems intent on leaving here with El Nino."

Just then the large front door opened and three desperados entered, each instinctively removing his sombrero. "Good afternoon, my friends," Padre de Escalante called out in his typically friendly voice as if greeting real friends.

"Good afternoon to you, Padre," Gustavo said, already feeling somewhat uncomfortable but yet determined to leave the building with fifty pounds of gold.

"Over the years, gentlemen," the padre said, "I've become quite adept at judging character, and intuition tells me that the three of you, not having confessed your sins and weaknesses for an extended period, simply couldn't bypass this sacred edifice without stopping to spend a moment or two in the confessional to unburden your weary hearts and souls. Am I right in this assessment?"

Temporarily disconcerted by these unexpected remarks, and not perceiving their sarcastic intent, Gustavo replied, "Padre, you **are** a keen judge of character, for to confess is part of our object in coming here. But in truth, it's a minor part of our errand. You see," and he peered all around the chapel area but saw no other person present, "you see, Padre, our errand is to leave here with the statue of El Nino. A higher power hath spoken to us, telling us to remove it hence so we can melt it down and put it to a much more effective use." His men's spontaneous laughter caused him to laugh with them. Even the padre laughed, titillated by the unconcealed brazenness.

"I knew it, gentlemen," the padre said matter of factly. "Just yesterday I commented to my assistant, Padre Ernesto, that today a band of armed and unprincipled rascals would be paying us a courtesy call, their real intent, however, being the removal of El Nino. Unfortunately, Padre Ernesto was called out of town on a personal matter and will certainly be disappointed to learn upon his return that you gentlemen have graced us with your scintillating presence. I am the only one who knows how to release the statue of El Nino from its mount, so may I assume that you will not be offended if I act as your---shall we say---tour guide? That is, I'll take the liberty of leading you up to look into the very eyes of El Nino, and after you've had the unforgettable experience of gazing, as it were, into the eyes of God's own Son, I'll explain how you can remove the statue from its mount. Incidentally, I wanted to comment briefly about your stated intent to melt down this incomparable work of art. Are you perchance aware that none other than world-renowned sculptor Luigi Arturo from Florence, Italy, the very home of the European Renaissance, traveled all the way over here to Mexico at considerable sacrifice to create this masterpiece? And you would cast his noble and humanitarian efforts to the wind just for the sake of filthy lucre?"

"Padre," Gustavo said somewhat sheepishly but without lessening his stated resolve, "we are not educated men like you. We are simple souls of the soil, the wind, the deserts, the forests, and the waste places of this vast and uncompromising land. Pray, how could **we** have developed any appreciation for art? Art means nothing to us. Asking us to appreciate art would be like asking swine to appreciate pearls. Money is what speaks our language, for with money comes power, and with power comes control over other people's lives. These are some of the reaons, Padre, why we are here. As for you, well, you've been blessed with the opportunity to view this statue from close up every day for a number of years, so I am told, and when we remove this statue, you will long remember what it looks like. Its image you will carry forever emblazoned on your heart. We, on the other hand, have no sentimental attachment to this piece of precious metal; hence, it will not affect any of us psychologically to see this block of gold melted down and reformed into one-half pound bars. . . ."

"I see," the padre said after listening intently to this little harangue, which was not totally devoid of its poetic elements. "In this case, then, perhaps you and I, Senor, should report to the confessional right over here while your two partners mosey on up to have a look at El Nino. And may I suggest, gentlemen, that you stand, both of you, right in front of the statue and take the opportunity of gazing directly into the eyes of that remarkable creation, which resulted from the spiritually guided hands of its illustrious creator? Go ahead, gentlemen. Your leader and I have a brief matter of business to attend to in the confessional."

Skillfully engineered into this little scenario, Gustavo followed the padre over to the confessional and stepped inside. "Make yourself comfortable, Senor," the padre said. "And, yes, just a simple request---please leave your pistols in the holsters. You see, it's not considered kosher for the penitent to sit in a holy confessional with weapons drawn."

"No problem, Padre," Gustavo said good naturedly and at the same time smiling at his own perceived cleverness.

Joining him on the other side of the confessional's partition, the padre reached inside his robe and withdrew a pistol and placed it on the little shelf in front of him. Meanwhile, Amado and Gilberto were preoccupied looking at and studying the statue of El Nino while visions of gold bars danced in their heads. In the confessional the padre opened the small round window to hear what would turn out to be a most interesting confession. Gustavo, letting himself be suckered into an untenable position, waited for the padre to declare himself ready to hear some highly questionable confessions. "And now, my son," Padre de Escalante began, "you have honored us this day with your presence and your stated intent to unburden yourself of all past wrongdoings. Where, good brother, would you like to begin the process of laying bare your heart before your Maker, before Him whose all-seeing eye looks directly into the very soul of every mother's son or daughter who walks this earth, this wondrous creation about which the spirit sons and daughters of God rejoiced when, as subsequently vouchsafed to the great and patient Job, He explained that an earth was a-preparing whereon these one day might dwell for the sole purpose of receiving a physical body and working out their eternal salvation? Yes, where, good brother, would you prefer to begin your expression of heartfelt sorrow for the more serious infractions of which we poor wretched mortals wallowing here in the shadow of death are guilty? As the prophet saith, 'To be carnally minded is death, but to be spiritually minded is life, yes, life eternal in its transcendent abundance, life everlasting in the very presence of

God and Christ and the vast concourses of holy angels and other resurrected beings worshiping at His throne. . . ."

At this instant when Gustavo was getting primed to confess ---if only this long-winded and flowery padre would shut up--- two muffled screams pierced the air. "What in the hell was that, padre!" Gustavo called out in alarm.

"Oh, 'twas a mere nothing, good brother. Merely an everyday occurrence when penitent souls stand before El Nino and gaze directly into the statue's eyes. Caught up in the ecstasy of the moment, people traditionally proclaim their pent-up spiritual emotion with shouts of pure joy such as you just heard from your two associates. Some have even been known to shout Hosannah! Do you think, good brother, that you likewise will shout in joyous accents when you stand in front of El Nino as your two partners just did? Undoubtedly you will. But first we must let you lay bare your soul before God. 'Tis true that He already sees directly and unimpededly into your soul, but we must remember that He has endowed us all with free agency and that, even though He knows our very thoughts, He still wants us to exercise our agency by confessing our sins and abominations. And if in our hearts and souls we truly have repented of all expressed wrongdoings, He in His ever-gracious way will forgive us our shortcomings and lovingly admonish us to refrain from repeating them evermore. Now, good brother, you already have stated that the main purpose of your present errand here in Ascension, and more particularly here in the Cathedral of Our Blessed Virgin, is to relieve this sacred edifice of El Nino, yes, great and incomparable El Nino, all fifty pounds of the purest gold of which El Nino is comprised, fifty pounds of the purest gold now made holy by its presence in this house of God, fifty pounds of pure gold contributed by the meek and lowly of the earth. It grieves my heart, yea verily, it **grieveth** my heart to contemplate the reality of this spiritual boon being removed from these sacred premises, where literally thousands have come to be healed by gazing with faith-filled eyes at the countenance of El Nino. But lo, you have expressed your irrevocable intent to remove this statue; and since you are a son of God endowed with free agency, I must lend you a neighborly hand in unlocking the statue from its mount so you can transport it away. God grant that I shall be forgiven for not interfering with the purpose of your errand. Indeed, when you stand before our Maker to give an accounting of your earthly stewardship, will you here and now promise me, hand over heart, that you'll not try to implicate me in any way whatsoever in this little---shall we say--- misdemeanor that you intend to carry out? Will you promise me, good brother?"

Both irritated and frustrated, Gustavo, now at the end of his patience, fairly exploded. "Padre, please pardon my candor, but you are full of horse crap! Never before this day have I ever heard such a spate of flowery nothings, one rowed against another. Do you never run down? I have the distinct impression that you could keep this idle talk going indefinitely. As for me, I don't have the patience or the time to listen to any more of your ramblings. Yes, let me confess here and now that it IS my intention to remove the statue of El Nino from this building. I don't place any credence in this El Nino bit. As far as I am concerned, that statue is nothing more and nothing less than a fifty-pound chunk of gold."

"But, good brother," the padre interrupted, "you as yet have not looked into the eyes of El Nino and felt the warmth of love, compassion, understanding, and HEALING emanating therefrom."

"To hell with all of that spiritual baloney, Padre! I'm here to remove that statue from this building, and I intend to carry out my plan. Moreover, I have the manpower outside to back me up if you or anyone else should be so foolish to interfere with our plans."

"So this is your stated purpose then?" the padre asked.

"Si, Senor, this IS my stated purpose. Now how in the hell can I make my intentions plainer than this?"

"And you are expecting the Father of us all to give the nod to His Beloved Son Jesus Christ, who voluntarily gave His very life to atone for the sins of all mankind---more specifically for those who repent of their personal sins---to forgive you of such a heinous crime as the removal of this sacred statue from this house of God, which God Himself has dedicated and consecrated

21

for the sole purpose of administering salvation to the souls of men? Tell me once again, good brother, if this is your implacable and undissuadable intent."

"It **IS**, Padre. Now I've had enough of this bullshit. I'm gittin outa this cubbyhole this very moment."

"But **wait**, good brother. Kindly do me the favor of placing your face against this mouthpiece and saying one last time, 'Yes, Padre, it **is** my intent to remove El Nino from this building.'"

"All right! All right! But that's it. After I say these words, I'm headin straight for that statue, where my men are waiting. Now listen to my final confession, Padre! I DO INTEND TO REMOVE . . ."

BANG! Pistol in hand, Padre de Escalante had just endowed Gustavo the bandit's forehead with a sudden surge of hot lead. And now Gustavo, quite dead, slumped to the floor. "Amado!" the padre called out. "Quick! Secure the front doors. Ernesto, have Sanchez fetch me one of those empty lime bags to keep this infidel from bleeding all over the place."

In short order Sanchez was there with the bag. "Amado, please come and help Sanchez carry this worthless piece of human flesh downstairs and drop it into the pit. First, though, remove his gunbelt and weapons and any extra ammunition he might be carrying. Also remove his boots. Some deserving soul can put them to better use. And, yes, drop another sack of lime down into the pit afterwards. Ernesto, please be so kind to fetch some soap and water and a couple rags so I can clean these few drops of blood from the confessional. It would look unseemly, you know, if some penitent soul came into this booth to confess his sins and saw blood. Course, we could explain that the last one in the confessional had demonstrated actual blood penitence!"

"Silvaro," Ernesto said laughing, "you are incorrigible. After creating you, God broke the mold!"

"Very likely true, Ernesto," Silvaro said smiling. "As you know, I am strictly a pragmatist. I do what needs to be done when it needs to be done. As for these three banditos who came here with blatantly expressed ill intent, I believe like an ancient prophet of whom I once read. Said he, after carrying out the command of God to terminate the earthly pilgrimage of one who was hearkening to the wrong spirit, 'It is better that one man perish than that a whole nation should dwindle in unbelief.' In our own case, it is far better that these worthless bandits be sent prematurely to the happy hunting grounds than to deprive the hundreds, yea, the thousands of souls of the great blessings of healing by exercising unwavering faith in God and Christ while looking upon El Nino, which statue is symbolical of God's own Son."

"The logic itself is unimpeachable, Silvaro. I only hope that God may sanction what we have just done. Incidentally, Amado is back up at his perch looking outside."

"Amado," Padre de Escalante called out, "are the rest of the banditos still there? Or do we have some unfinished business left?"

"They've disappeared, padre, apparently gone with the wind. However, several groups of worshipers are now approaching the building."

"Please unbolt the front doors, son."

Presently the cathedral began to fill with worshipers, among them many who had not come on their own power. "Good afternoon, brethren and sisters," the friendly padre said, revealing his much envied glistening white teeth in a smile that said, "Life is good."

PANCHO VILLA COMES A-CALLING

At the bandito headquarters, General Villa, gunbelt strapped on and two bands of cartridges crisscrossed over his chest, puffed a big black cigar incessantly as he paced back and forth. "What the hell could have happened to Gustavo and his men?" he asked, speaking to no one in particular. "They should have been back here by now with some fifty pounds of gold. Surely they would have encountered little opposition from a couple of friars. . . . Or might they have absconded with the loot?"

Just then a cloud of dust appeared on the horizon. "That must be them now," he said looking much relieved and breaking into a broad smile. "Gentlemen," he then exclaimed ecstatically, "ever seen **fifty** pounds of gold before? Well, you're about to see a fifty-pound hunk just as soon as them fellers come ridin in."

"General," one of the men said, a note of alarm in his voice, "I count only five men, which means that something has happened to the other five."

"Don't jump to conclusions, Manuel," Villa said, trying to be calm. "The other five will have good reasons for not being in this group."

Presently the five riders, all looking sheepish, dismounted and walked slowly up to Villa, who stood there looking both expectant and worried. "Well, **speak**, damn it! Ruben, what 'n the hell's been goin on? Where's them five other men?"

Head ducked slightly, Ruben Garcia proceeded timidly to explain. "General Villa," he said in a subdued voice, "we honestly don't know what happened to them."

"You WHAT! You DON'T KNOW WHAT HAPPENED TO THEM! WHAT IN THE NAME OF HADES IS GOIN ON, RUBEN? DID YOU FALL ASLEEP UP THERE? DID THE PRIEST COME OUT AND HYPNOTIZE YOU? WHAT IN THE SAM HELL HAPPENED ANYWAY? DON'T JUST STAND THERE WITH YOUR FINGER IN YOUR REAR END! I WANT SOME ANSWERS AND WANT THEM **RIGHT NOW**! WHERE'S THEM OTHER FELLERS? SPEAK UP, RUBEN! WHERE'D THEY GO? SURELY YOU

HAVE AT LEAST SOME INKLING OF THEIR WHEREABOUTS!"

No concrete answer was forthcoming from the five chagrined men. Finally Ruben, noting the general's mounting anger, felt it wise to attempt some kind of explanation. "General Villa, Sir," he said humbly, "when we arrived at the Cathedral of the Holy Virgin, Gustavo asked Francisco and Juan to go in and have a look around, which they did. But that's the last we saw of them. Then after ten or fifteen minutes Gustavo sent Carlos and Roberto in to check on them. They returned after about eight or ten minutes, their faces pale as if they'd seen a ghost or something. 'Gustavo,' they said, unable to conceal their embarrassment, 'something weird's goin on in that place. We decided that it was in our best interests to git the hell outa there.' Then Gustavo said, 'Well, what **happened** to Francisco and Juan?' 'We really don't know, Gustavo,' they said. 'The padre, a friendly though strange sort of fellow, said they'd been invited downstairs to eat some kind of bread and to drink some red wine before being able to remove the statue from its mount."

"Carlos," Pancho Villa asked, his face growing redder with anger, for he was known to have a violent temper and a short fuse, "is this bullshit I've just been hearing true? **Did you and Roberto** actually behave like a couple of addle brains? I've always thought of you as two of my best men. How could you have have conducted yourselves in such a disgraceful manner? Huh? What in the hell's goin on anyway?"

Ruben, attempting a further explanation, said, "General Villa, at this point Gustavo took Ramon and Gilberto with him. They did not return as Gustavo promised they would. Then we heard a muffled shot. We were about to rush in when Carlos and Roberto said, 'Men, something absolutely mysterious is goin on in that damned place. You'd have to hog-tie us to git us back in there.' When I suggested that we go in and see if those men were in difficulty of some kind, I looked around just as these fellers were giving their horses the spurs. Why, hell, General, we didn't even take time to bring them other horses back with us. Course, on second thought it was good that we didn't, assuming that them fellers eventually made it outa the church alive."

"Made it outa the church ALIVE!" Villa said mockingly. "What in tarnation's goin on up there anyway?" Hearing no further explanations, he said, "I'll tell you fellers one thing right now. We're headin up that way before daybreak tomorrow morning. I'm gonna git to the root of this bizarre situation if it's the last thing I do!" He kept his promise.

Next day shortly before noon Villa and some twenty-five or thirty men came riding into Ascension, their specific destination the Cathedral of the Blessed Virgin. Worshipers could be seen both coming and going. Many who had been carried into the cathedral came walking out on their own power, their faces suffused with inexpressible joy. Seeing the notorious general and his men, however, the crowd started to disperse; and, at the behest of the two priests, worshipers inside the building quickly began to exit the premises by the side doors. Padre Ernesto then assumed his usual battle station, and Amado went quickly to his perch by the upper window. Sanchez, too, was observing the proceedings from a concealed place where he could move posthaste to the lever controlling the trapdoor if necessary.

Outside, Villa was gloating over the fear that his presence had instilled into the hearts of the many worshipers. "Look at all o' them dumb bastards," he said smiling. "You can rest assured that they know what's good for 'em. That's why they're scattering like a bunch o' rabbits." Selecting some of his most trusted followers, the general said, "The rest of you men wait out here with your weapons ready, and keep an eye on these horses. Don't let any of them git away. Us fellers are goin in to straighten that joint out once and for all. I'm fed up with all this pussyfootin and piddlin around."

Padre de Escalante was more than halfway down one of the aisles leading to the front doors when they swung open. Pancho Villa, flamboyant, self-assured, his pistols drawn, and about twenty heavily armed men following, entered the building. The unflappable padre, tall, handsome, suave, athletically built, and in his mid-thirties, smiled graciously as if greeting old friends. "A most pleasant good morning, gentlemen! And to you, General Villa, a special good morning! To what may we attribute this signal honor if I might be so bold to ask? And, by the way,

27

gentlemen, unless you take me, a lone man, for some kind of super magician, you may feel free to replace your weapons in their holsters. Oh, and one other small favor, kindly remove your hats----as I note that some of you already have done. After all, this **is** the house of the LORD, and divine etiquette requires that we gentlemen remove our headpieces whenever we enter these sacred premises. Now, General, forgive my long welcoming address. What might we do for you this morning?"

"Padre," Villa began, "let me say at the outset that I'm not much on ceremony. I make it a practice of gittin right to the point, right to the heart of the matter. Now, I'd like you to tell me, Padre, what happened to five of my men who entered this cathedral yesterday afternoon."

"Seven men, General. Two of them, whom I recognize in this very group, came in and visited for a few minutes, actually only long enough to take a serious look at El Nino from close range. Both of them commented on how strange they felt when looking directly into El Nino's eyes. Then the first thing I knew they were hightailing it out of the building, in effect leaving me in mid-sentence."

"Yes, yes, Padre, I've heard about all that crap already. Now I want you to tell me candidly what happened to the other five."

"Well, Sir," the padre continued, "the first two graciously accepted our kind invitation to go down to the dining room in the basement to partake of some shewbread and red wine. It is so very seldom that we are able to offer anyone a bit of physical nourishment here in the cathedral. By and large, the kind of nourishment we offer is spiritual in nature. Shewbread, such as was offered anciently to David and his band of followers, was what we offered the two men. The other three, for reasons that we as yet haven't fathomed, chose not to partake. However, they did walk up front to have a close look at El Nino, which one of them, Gustavo I think he said his name was, intended to remove from its mount and to take it out to your headquarters for melting down and converting into half-pound bars. Since this statue weighs fifty pounds, pure gold all of it, that would make some one hundred bars---a remarkable treasure in anyone's language, would you not agree, General Villa?"

"Course I'd agree, Padre. Do you take me for an idiot? Course I'd agree."

"Anyway, General, these five men insisted that they had some unfinished business just across the border in that little gringo town of Columbus. One of the men, joking about their excuse for heading up there, said something about women they needed to see."

"<u>WOMEN</u> THEY NEEDED TO SEE!" Villa bellowed. "Why, those rotten sonsab---. Oh, pardon me, Padre, but I cautioned them fellers in no uncertain terms NOT to go lolligaggin after women up there anymore. And, dadblast it, they all gave me their word."

"Yes, I know, General. As the great English playwright William Shakespeare has Falstaff, one of his most famous character creations, say, 'It's a sad thing when thieves can't trust one another!' If memory serves me correctly, money was also the central issue in that make-believe situation."

"Did I detect a slight insinuation in your observation, Padre?" Villa asked, a smile stealing over his face.

Unruffled, the padre, likewise smiling, replied, "Well, General, all seven of your men came in here telling me quite candidly that their intent was to remove the statue of El Nino from these sacred premises. And the five that made the little detour up across the border said they'd call for the statue on their way back. Always the gracious host, I told them that if this was their sincere intent, I'd be happy to show them how to unlock the mechanism that holds the statue to its mount. After all, how could I, a lone man---my assistant not having returned from visiting his very ill mother---even make a show of contending with several heavily armed men? Hence, it would be in my personal best interests to assist them in removing El Nino."

"The hell you say!" Villa said laughing. "The hell you say! Am I awake or dreaming? It's one or the other, and if not, then you, Padre, must be full of prunes. You sound rational and yet you don't. It's no secret that my intention is to remove this statue---fifty pounds of pure gold---and convert it into gold bars, a hundred or so of them. One helluva lot of power that'll place directly into my hands, wouldn't you say, Padre?" Villa

29

appeared to be enjoying this little verbal cat and mouse game, for he was fully confident that he and his men would be leaving here with the statue.

"Indeed it would, General. To be honest with you, the thought of making off with this statue once crossed my own mind, but that was before this masterpiece had been completed by world-renowned sculptor Luigi Arturo from Florence, Italy. After taking my first look at it---in fact, after my first look at the plaster of paris model he created to make the mold for the statue itself---I changed my mind. Then after seeing the consummately finished product in gold, yes, in all its transcendent splendor, I definitively changed my mind. Truthfully, it would be far easier for me to jump off the highest cliff I could find than it would be to confiscate this magnificent statue. Looking directly into the eyes of this masterpiece is tantamount to looking into the actual eyes of Christ. You see, a power emanates from the statue; and as a result of this power and the unwavering faith of the hundreds, nay, the thousands, who have come here to be healed of physical, mental, and spiritual maladies, I know that a power far greater than any found on earth is at play here. Quite obviously you have your free agency, General Villa, to confiscate this consummate work of art, this healer of the sick, the halt, the maimed, the lame, the congenitally crippled---you name them. But my humble assessment of such an atrocious act is that you would pay a hefty price, far greater than you would want to pay---once you found yourself on the spiritual hotseat."

"You're a convincing fellow, Padre," Villa said, then stole a glance at his men. All heads nodded affirmatively. "Yes, Padre, you've introduced an element of doubt in my mind. But don't misread me. I'm not saying as yet that I've changed my mind. We still might ride off with this statue."

"And would you, my dear General, do that at the risk of unleashing a searing fire within your breast, a fire comparable to thrusting a white-hot poker inside your chest and smelling your own flesh sizzling?"

"Padre, I think you're trying to hoo-doo me with some juvenile scare tactics."

"Look at your men, General. I perceive that they believe there may be more truth than fiction in what I've been saying. Go ahead. Ask some of them how they feel about removing this statue from here."

"That won't be necessary, Padre. Do you want me to look like a wet dishrag in front of my men? If I did that, they'd lose whatever respect they have for me. But I will say one thing, Padre. You've piqued my interest about looking at that statue. Before we go I'd like to see it, and I'm sure my men also would want to see it so they can judge the situation themselves. Is this agreeable to you, Padre?"

"By all means, General. Simply follow me if you would, please." Approaching the statue, with Pancho Villa right behind, Padre de Escalante said, "Here we are, my dear General. Now if you dare risk it, look directly into the eyes of El Nino and then tell me how you feel."

Studying this incomparable work of art for a few seconds, Villa suddenly turned away, his eyes feeling as if they were on fire. "I must have gotten something in my eyes, Padre," the general said, and then proceeded to remove whatever it was, or appeared to be, from his eyes.

His men, some of them timidly, stepped forward to have a look at the statue. One of them, a large man with a handlebar mustache and a quid of chewing tobacco in his mouth, said, "Men, I'm not afraid of no damned statue. This thing's not alive. It's just a hunk of metal shaped in the figure of a person." And thus speaking, he reached up and slapped El Nino to the side of the head. "See that!" he laughed. "This stupid thing aint got no power at all; its just a figment of people's imagination. Right, General?" Then he reached up to to slap the other side of El Nino but didn't quite make it. The trapdoor suddenly opened and, like lightning, he dropped out of sight, apparently so startled that he couldn't even get his mind in gear to scream. No sooner had the trapdoor opened till it closed again, leaving not so much as a trace of its even being there.

"DID YOU SEE <u>THAT</u>!" Padre de Escalante gasped, acting as if his breath had just been knocked out. Those who had witnessed this episode stood there white as ghosts. "I don't know

31

about you, gentlemen," the startled padre said, "but I'm getting out of here. This is far more dangerous than I myself had imagined." Having delivered his lines superbly, he turned and made a dash for one of the side doors with twenty or so banditos following and Pancho Villa, quite out of breath, bringing up the rear. Caught up in this drama, the padre staged a first-class performance outside the cathedral, the paleness of his face accentuated by the blackness of his robe. As for the men, they headed posthaste for their waiting horses and, quickly swinging up into their saddles, soon had spurred their horses into a dead run.

"Padre!" a breathless Pancho Villa paused to say to de Escalante, "I don't know what the hell's goin on here at this damned place, but if I decide to return to remove that confounded statue from the premises, it will be with a fully equipped army. Don't rule out this possibility." Then running with spurs jingling, he vaulted into the saddle and proceeded to follow his men, all of whom had absconded like scared rabbits.

From a distance various worshipers looked on in utter disbelief. The news of this bizarre occurrence soon spread like wildfire, and thereafter all who entered the Cathedral of the Blessed Virgin did so with increased reverence bordering on fear.

Re-entering the cathedral while struggling to control his laughter, Padre Silvaro de Escalante saw Padre Ernesto, the boy Amado, and Sanchez standing together, faces white. "Sanchez," de Escalante said half laughing, "which of these guys gave you the signal to open the trapdoor at that precise moment?"

"Padre," Sanchez said in the soberest of tones, "no one gave me the signal. I was merely standing there by the lever when all of a sudden the trapdoor opened and closed in an instant suddenly. I saw a bandito flailing his arms but making no sound as he zoomed downward and crashed with a mighty thud at the bottom of the pit. Dutifully I crossed myself and then dumped another sack of lime into the pit."

Momentarily speechless, the now much sobered Padre de Escalante gulped hard and went very pale, this time involuntarily pale. Catching his breath and collecting his wits, he finally spoke. "Gentlemen, rarely am I at a loss for words, but at this moment I'm not entirely sure how I should respond to what has just transpired. A power much greater than any of us can know is emanating from El Nino. Needless to say, this magnificent statue has been the conduit through which unnumbered blessings have come to hundreds, perhaps even to thousands, for they have been healed according to their faith, and indeed the faith of those having barely perceptible faith at the outset has been strengthened, sometimes immeasurably. But it now is clear to all of us that such a fabulous prize as El Nino is going to inspire repeated attempts by individuals, groups, even armies, to attack this place, which will mean constant confrontations with the rabble who get it into their hollow heads that they are going to steal fifty pounds of solid gold. But our greatest worry, quite obviously, is Villa. That scoundrel is very determined; and if I'm reading the tea leaves correctly, he will return with enough men to tear down this building stone by stone if necessary to get the gold. Anyway, what has happened here these past couple days inspires me to voice what has been on my mind for quite some time. Until this revolutionary spirit and general political unrest come to an end, I wonder if we ought not to pack this statue in clay and transport it up over the U. S. border, naturally unbeknown to the authorities or to anyone else for that matter. Up in New Mexico near the border with Arizona is a sacred cave just north of Camarra, where we could take El Nino for temporary safekeeping. No one other than the four of us would ever know what had happened to the statue until peace finally prevails in Mexico and it will be safe to bring El Nino back to this cathedral."

"Silvaro," Ernesto said, "I'm impressed with this proposed solution. El Nino definitely must **not** remain here in Mexico. We must remove the temptation altogether, which means secretly transporting the statue up over the border until, as you suggest, the political climate in this troubled area has calmed down. For the time being we could say that El Nino simply had vanished. The faithful will be inclined to regard this as another miracle among many."

"I go along with what both of you have said," Sanchez told them. "Indeed, if I can be of help in transporting the statue to its desired location, I'll be glad to volunteer."

"Thank you, Sanchez," de Escalante said. "You're a trustworthy friend, our faithful Achates. We will put you in charge of this special project; then after the political situation has stabilized in Mexico, we'll appoint you to go and fetch El Nino back to Ascension, back here to this our beautiful Cathedral of the Blessed Virgin. In doing this I feel that we have the personal approbation of the Blessed Virgin herself, for surely she has a vested interest in El Nino."

EL NINO CROSSES THE U. S. BORDER

Within days the statue, safely and skillfully packed in clay, was on its way into the United States of America, Sanchez and two assistants posing as prospectors. Each one rode a mule while two burros carried their camping gear, the picks and shovels, and of course El Nino. Sticking exclusively to wilderness areas, they managed to avoid contact with people, some of whom would have ended up asking questions and demanding answers.

Padre de Escalante had outfitted each man with a high-powered rifle, two pistols, and a thousand rounds of ammunition. "Hermanos," he had said to them, "Vaya con Dios, for God will protect you and El Nino. As a backup, however, Ernesto and I thought it wisdom to provide you with some firepower if the need should arise. These are revolutionary times, and many rough and tough hombres from these parts skip up over the border from time to time whether by personal choice or sheer necessity to stay a step or two ahead of the law. Oftentimes they cross over just to raise hell. Other times they might have women on their minds. But whatever their reasons might be, you must be on the lookout at all times. But Mexicanos on the rampage are not your only problems; there are many lawless characters among the Norteamericanos. Moreover, various Indians such as Comanches and Apaches are often on the loose in the area you'll be traversing. You are bound to encounter some excitement; and the more I think about it, the more I wish I were going with you. However, my ecclesiastical duties do not permit me to indulge. But for what it's worth, our thoughts and prayers will be with you. Remember now that you are heading for Camarra, which is a hundred or so miles up into New Mexico and very close to the border with Arizona. If memory serves me correctly, some two miles or so north of Camarra and next to a peculiar-looking hill called Molly's Nipple you'll find some caves. Use your judgment as to which one you select for the temporary hiding place for El Nino; and take special precautions that no one sees you near the place. Be ingenious, Sanchez, in the manner in which you deposit El Nino in the cave. I need not say that it should be in a manner that no one would suspect. In fine, the specific tactics we leave up to you. Then as soon as the political unrest dies down sufficiently and the ardor of the revolutionaries has dissipated, we'll set about retrieving El Nino to begin once again the marvelous, indeed wondrous, healing process that up to this time has brought so much happiness to so many lives. . . ."

So the little party of three men, three mules, and two burros began the arduous journey toward Camarra. Each of the three felt a bit of apprehension, and yet they were confident of being able to complete this important mission; in effect, they were placing El Nino far enough away from the political turmoil that regardless how hard the rabble might seek, they in nowise would ever come close to finding the precious statue.

They left at midnight and in the dark of the moon so that none of the townspeople would be aware of their departure, for tongues naturally would have wagged if the little three-man expedition had been seen.

"Well, Julio and Jose," Sanchez said somewhat jocularly to them, "how do you feel about this big adventure we're on? Are you afraid? Excited? Happy? Just how do you feel anyway?"

"Perhaps all of these things to one degree or another, Sanchez," Julio said with a chuckle. "I've always wanted to get away for more than just two or three days when we've gone hunting in the mountains, and this would appear to be the fulfillment of my wish."

"And you, Jose?" Sanchez asked.

"Oh, I feel more or less like Julio. It's big adventure, and I feel especially complimented that the two padres have such faith and confidence in us to entrust us with El Nino, which after all weighs fifty or so pounds, all pure gold. But, you see, I've witnessed so many miracles wrought by El Nino that any thought of not carrying out the specific assignment that we have been given is totally out of the question. In short, I'm prepared to lay my life on the line to protect El Nino, for God has manifested Himself again and again by means of this beautiful piece of sculpture, which in many respects seems to have a life of its own."

"Those are very noble sentiments, Jose," Sanchez said. "Do you not think so, too, Julio?"

"Most certainly I do. Jose has formed into words the very things I have been thinking. I deem it a privilege to have such faith and trust placed in me."

"That makes three of us," Sanchez added. "I'm sure we'll all be better men in a variety of ways when we can return to our wives and children in Ascension after the successful completion of our---shall we not say---'prospecting mission'?"

PANCHO VILLA PAYS ANOTHER VISIT

The next day Pancho Villa and some 150 heavily armed men, a veritable army for those times and conditions, converged upon the humble little town of Ascension. The townspeople, however, noting their approach, quickly made themselves scarce, leaving the streets wanting for human habitation. Given Villa's reputation for brutality, none of the citizenry wanted to become entangled in any way whatsoever with him. Villa's destination---need it be said?---was the Cathedral of the Blessed Virgin. It being about 9:30 in the morning, small groups of the faithful could be seen approaching the cathedral from the opposite end of town, some of them carrying their sick and afflicted.

Becoming aware of the banditos, however, all of these humble souls did an abrupt about-face and headed in the direction whence they had come. Smiling, Villa said to those closest to him, "Well, men, apparently we won't have much of an audience when we ride off with El Nino. Now, the thirty of you that I've hand-picked are to come with me to pay what might be termed a courtesy call on silver-tongued Padre de Escalante. One has to be extremely alert around this veritable wizard of words."

Inside the cathedral Ernesto, Amado, and Sanchez's younger brother Emilio were at their specified places, Padre de Escalante having coached them on what to do when Villa and his men showed up, which he said would be within days. Walking slowly down the left-hand aisle in anticipation of Villa's entry (for Amado had been apprising the padre of their movements out front), de Escalante, calm, self-possessed, and eager, awaited their entrance into the cathedral. Suddenly the doors were swung open to accommodate the banditos, their flamboyant general at the head of the pack. Sombrero in hand and smiling broadly as if about to greet an old friend, he approached.

Getting the jump on him, de Escalante, smiling and exuding supreme confidence, said, "A fine good morning to you, General Villa, and to your cohorts!"

"And a good morning to you, my Friend," Villa said as if the relationship between them were both amicable and long-lived. "Did I not tell you, Padre, that I would return? And all the time you thought the hokus-pokus that you hoo-dooed me with would have changed my mind."

"General," de Escalante said still smiling, "you're quite right. I knew that the spiritual effect would wear off in a matter of days. Are you not like some of the rebellious spirits that Moses had the challenge of leading out of Egypt and out onto that forbidding piece of real estate called the Sinai Peninsula, where they sojourned for some forty years until all of the old dogs had died off? For verily, some old dogs simply cannot be taught new tricks, can they?"

"Quite right, padre," Villa said chuckling. "Quite right. And I do not take offense at being referred to, if only symbolically, as an old dog, for I suppose that characterizes me about as accurately as anyone has attempted thus far, at least in my presence. But as you know, Padre, I am not a sophisticated and highly educated man like you, and I know that any attempt on my part to match wits with you would place me rather quickly in an untenable position. For, you see, I am at heart just a simple man, a man of the waste places, of the sun and the rain and the wind, a veritable son of the soil, if I may say so. Unlike you, padre, I am not trained to deal in abstractions but rather in concrete realities; and El Nino," he said, pausing to laugh good-naturedly with the padre joining in, "is a concrete---or shall we not say a GOLD---reality!"

"Very clever, my dear General, very clever indeed, and not without a touch of poetry."

"Well, thank you, Padre, for the kind words. I take them as a genuine compliment, especially coming from you. But, Padre, smooth-tongued though you may be, not a second time will I let you talk me out of leaving these premises without El Nino, which translates into some fifty pounds of pure gold. Do I make myself sufficiently clear, my dear Padre de Escalante?"

"Crystal clear, my dear General. But I'll tell you what. If you're up to it, I'll wager you a pound of gold that you do NOT leave here today with El Nino!"

"The hell you say, Padre!" Villa said laughing uproariously. "Surely you have not taken leave of your senses! I have thirty heavily armed men right here in the cathedral with me and over a hundred more waiting just outside. It would be the height of idiocy on your part to try to stop me from riding off with El Nino."

"General, I trust that you recall the incident when---if you'll pardon my last reference to the ancient Israelites---the incident when the Ark of the Covenant was about to tip over and a well-meaning, albeit unauthorized, fellow sprang forward to steady that sacred object and, upon touching it, was literally fried to a crisp when the equivalent of some 50,000 volts shot through him. Moses played that incident to the hilt, leaving no doubt in anyone's mind that unholy hands should not touch holy objects. Now, General, does the point of this little story connect with you?"

"Look, Padre, I know that, given the chance, you could talk the leaves off the trees, but I'm not going to let myself be pulled into one of your clever verbal traps as I was the other day. I am here to confiscate this fifty-pound statue, and no one is going to stop me. I need money to pay my troops, and what better way to do so than to melt down that statue and pay each man his rightful share?"

"Tell me, General," the padre asked with a smile, "do you personally intend to touch El Nino?"

"You can bet your last peso, my dear Padre, that I'm going to touch it!"

"And would you risk such a thing after getting your eyes seared a bit the other day by just looking at the statue, let alone touching it?"

"That's precisely what I intend to do, Padre. Now let's put an end to the fluff and foam and bubbles here and get right down to the Khyber rifles, so to speak. Men! . . ."

"Just a moment, General," de Escalante said. "I beg your pardon for interrupting so uncouthly, but with your permission I'd like a brief word with your men. I want to ask them a simple question that bears on you, their trusted and respected leader."

41

Eyeing the priest impatiently for a moment, Villa said, "All right. Go ahead. But there will be NO MORE DELAYS after this one."

"Thank you, General." Then addressing himself specifically to Villa's increasingly perplexed men, the padre said, "Gentlemen, I have a simple question or two for you to consider most seriously, for this IS a serious matter. When General Villa stretches forth his arm to touch El Nino and is fried to a crisp, which one of you will pray at his grave? Which one of you will offer the eulogy? Which one of you will sing an holy hymn for the general? Have you perchance thought about these things?"

Not a man stirred. Villa himself broke the silence. "C'mon, Padre. Surely you can't be serious about this nonsense?"

"Dead serious, General. Have you so soon forgotten that when you were standing near the statue the other day one of your men, a big macho man displaying unwonted bravado by reaching up and slapping El Nino, suddenly dropped right out of sight--- indeed, right before your very eyes and the eyes of your men? I myself was so shocked that I hightailed it out of the building, yes, shocked right down to the marrow of my bones; and you yourself, General, if you will pardon my candor, were practically trampling me to get outside and onto your horse. And if you again will pardon me for saying so, General Villa, I couldn't help finding it amusing, despite the seriousness of the occasion, that your men rode off leading YOU instead of you leading THEM! So now you are getting all primed to have your men carry your blackened remains out of the building this time! AM I RIGHT, GENERAL?"

"I'm willing to risk it, Padre. After all, we're practically old friends!"

"I concur with those sentiments, General; for I must admit that I do feel a certain affinity for you. Indeed, under other circumstances it is not inconceivable that you and I could become **great** friends. This fact prompts me to say that in my ten years and El Nino's four years at this post in Ascension I have seen literally hundreds of sick and afflicted souls healed of their maladies. A number of these pathetic human beings were congenital cripples carried here on stretchers; miraculously they

42

left on their own power, all of them standing straight and tall as young elms. Practically every day here I see similar scenes, similar miracles. It's gotten to the point where people even from foreign countries have started coming here. Our humble little town of Ascension is now on the map, not just on the Mexican map but rather on the world map. There is even some talk about His Holiness the Pope paying us a visit sometime next year. General, surely in your more sober moments you wouldn't want to go down in history as the one individual who spoiled all of this, would you?"

"Padre," Villa said, his face belying an unmistakable sense of frustration, "I came here this morning all primed to remove this confounded statue, and again---**against** my wishes---you've bamboozled me into an untenable position. How in the hell do you do it anyway? Every time I git around you I can't even think straight!"

Right at this precise moment one of Villa's lieutenants, glancing in the direction of El Nino, or rather where El Nino had been, exclaimed in alarm: "GENERAL! THAT STATUE JUST DISAPPEARED! I SWEAR THAT I SAW IT WHEN WE ENTERED THIS BUILDING, BUT IT JUST NOW DISAPPEARED!"

Villa, quickly looking in that direction, said, "Madre de Dios, it IS gone! And I, too, saw it as soon as we came in here. What in the name of Father, Son, and Holy Ghost and all holy angels is going on in this damned place anyway!"

Padre de Escalante likewise looked in the direction of where El Nino had been and, consummate actor that he was, turned pale, gasped for breath, and staggered slightly as if about to fall. Villa and his men were visibly affected by the statue's disappearance and by the padre's superb histrionics. Turning to Villa, the padre said, "General, this **CAN'T** BE! WHY, NOT MORE THAN TWENTY MINUTES AGO I STOOD GAZING AT THAT INCOMPARABLE WORK OF ART AND WONDERING HOW MUCH LONGER EL NINO WOULD GRACE THIS EDIFICE. AND NOW HE IS **GONE!**"

As tears welled up in the padre's eyes, several of Villa's men quickly crossed themselves while their leader stood there not knowing what to do or say. With Villa and his men following close behind, the padre led the way up to the stand where El Nino had been mounted. The stand, having been restored to its natural state by Sanchez, no marks of any kind could be discovered indicating that the statue had ever occupied that spot. "General Villa," the padre said quite out of breath, "not more than twenty or so minutes ago the statue of El Nino rested right here on this very mount, which was created for that sole purpose. Another miracle has occurred, for I am speechless! Either God Himself or the Holy Mother has removed this statue. There's simply no other explanation. Do you realize, General, what this means?"

"Yes, Padre, I do," Villa said in subdued tones. "It means that I'm out of fifty pounds of gold!"

"No, General," the padre countered while struggling to control the almost overpowering urge to laugh, "not that! It means that God has wrought this miracle to spare YOUR life. You are an important person, General. But if you had actually touched El Nino, you'd have been reduced to a heap of ashes in a split second. General Villa, may I humbly suggest that you look up and say a BIG THANK YOU to the Father of us all! You truly are an important man, General, for God has seen fit to spare your life. Like Hezekiah of old, you have just been granted some extra years of life. Do you realize, Sir, that news of this miracle will spread like wildfire throughout this entire region and beyond?"

Villa himself was still speechless, and all of his men, again crossing themselves, appeared to be taken in completely by the padre's inimitable theatrics. Visibly disturbed but finally able to speak, Villa said, "Padre, I honestly do not know what to say about all of this. I knew when I came back here that I shouldn't have let myself get locked into a conversation with you. You're not a padre; you're a wizard of some kind. I wouldn't be at all surprised if you yourself, through some kind of hokus-pokus, didn't make that statue disappear into thin air." Then turning to his troops, Pancho Villa said, "MEN, I'VE BEEN THOROUGHLY HUMILIATED! Let's git outa this damnable place before we look down and find ourselves standing here buck naked! I don't trust this padre anymore!"

Villa and his men, faces red and spurs jingling, quickly exited the building and sheepishly joined their companeros to ride off in a big cloud of dust.

In the Cathedral of the Blessed Virgin the walls echoed with uproarious laughter, for Padre de Escalante had just pulled off the stunt of the century. "Gentlemen," he said, "let the word go forth that God, for reasons known only to Himself, hath removed the statue of El Nino to spare the life of that villain Pancho Villa! When the political situation has died down and Villa has either mellowed or been brought to heel, we'll retrieve El Nino and proclaim that God in His infinite wisdom has seen fit to restore El Nino to his rightful place here in the Cathedral of the Blessed Virgin. As for the healings, behold, they will continue. So much has happened here---yea, the things that legends are made of--- that people's faith will actually increase. Indeed, whereas prior to this day El Nino was the sacred shrine, henceforth this cathedral itself will be a shrine to which pilgrims even from faraway lands will come to worship and to be healed of divers afflictions, be they physical, spiritual, or both. Yes, people everywhere will say that El Nino once graced this place and in the Lord's own due time will grace it again. O the goodness of God! . . ."

DESTINATION CAMARRA

On the trail Sanchez and company had traveled some fifty miles up into New Mexico, all the while veering off in a westerly direction since Camarra lay very close to Arizona's eastern border. The terrain was varied, for in addition to vast stretches of cacti, they had begun to encounter patches of pines as they moved ever higher into the mountains.

Thus far they had encountered no one although twice they had gotten a glimpse of what appeared to be hunters off in the distance. But now, just as they came up over the crest of a grassy knoll, they ran smack dab into a party of four hunters, young men in their mid-twenties and early thirties. Turning sharply to the left to avoid having to speak with the gringos, they had gone but fifteen or twenty yards when one of the hunters addressed them.

"Hey, Mexicanos! What in the hell do you think you're doing up here anyway? Are you lost? Don't you know you're trespassing?"

Paying no attention to the gringos, they continued on their way when again the same rowdy person accosted them in unfriendly tones. HEY, you friggin numbskulls, I'm talkin to you, and I expect an answer. What in the hell are you a doin up in these parts? Don't you know this is not Mexico? This is the United States of America, which means you are trespassing."

Sanchez, who had spent a couple years working in Columbus, New Mexico, and had made a concerted effort to learn English, even going to great lengths to be tutored in the language, said, "Yes, gentlemen, it's true that we're Mexicans and that we're in the United States. We're on our way to Camarra, where we have important business to transact. Our means of locomotion is obviously slow and occasionally tedious; therefore, time is of the essence, so we hereby bid you gentlemen a Good Day so we can proceed on our way." Under his breath Sanchez said to his partners, "Let's keep moving. These are some bad hombres." They had just started on their way again when the same big mouth brayed again.

47

"Hold it right there, hermanos! We're not through with you."

Slightly riled by this brazenness and assumed superiority, Sanchez said, "You say **you're** not through with us? What in the hell would **you** have to do with us? And who, pray tell, has endowed **you** with any authority over us? Are you suggesting that, unlike normal men, you stand while putting your pants on both legs at the same time?"

At this, one of big mouth's partners said, "Well, what d'ya know? We've got us a smart-ass Mexican mouthing off to us!"

"Fella," Sanchez said, "the smart asses are clearly on your side, as the remarks from both of you hombres prove. We were merely passing by while minding our business. You accosted us. We had no intention of disturbing your reverie, and we'd appreciate the same display of courtesy from you. Or might that be asking too much, gentlemen?"

"As a matter of fact it would, peon! And how did you learn to speak English like that? You don't even sound like a Mexican."

"Frankly, I don't see that my linguistic abilities should be any concern of yours. Now Good Day, gentlemen."

"Hold it! I said HOLD it! You're not leaving here till we tell you to leave, Mexican, and as yet we haven't told you."

To his men Sanchez said, "Let's go. Ignore the simple-minded bastard." As they started to move again, a shot rang out, and a bullet richocheted near them, scaring their animals. They stopped. Four men, weapons drawn, were moving toward them.

Big mouth started to bray again. "Since you know English so well, didn't you see that I was speaking to you, you low-down peon?"

"Yes, I saw you, but seeing you alarmed me---I couldn't tell for sure if it was your mouth or your ass you were speaking from! I'm sure that a simple comparison would reveal some remarkable similarities between the two."

"Why, you son of a buck!" big mouth said. "I ought to shoot you right here on the spot."

"What's the matter, fella," Sanchez said, "do you have an aversion to the truth? Now if it's all the same to you gentlemen, we have important business in Camarra to tend to."

"You have 'important business in Camarra,' do you?" big mouth said sarcastically. "I'll bet you're like the rest of them friggin bean eaters south of the border. You eat beans every Saturday night so you can have a bubble bath Sunday morning!" The three other gringos laughed uproariously at their partner's ribald humor. Egged on by their show of support, big mouth continued. "We've just decided that you three cocky little roosters aren't going anywhere."

"Tell me, fatso," Sanchez said, "might your wee brain be big enough to suggest to you that you're getting yourself into a predicament with rapidly diminishing returns for you and your compadres?" Then before big mouth could formulate a response, Sanchez said, "You four big brave men are standing there with drawn weapons. If it's a fight you're looking for, I'll be happy to take you on one at a time---or even two at a time if you're not macho enough to take me one at a time. This must be without weapons, of course. I warn you, however, that I've had considerable specialized training in a new discipline called the martial arts and have distinguished myself as an instructor in the same. So if like good little boys you'll kindly put your weapons away as befitting gentlemen, I'll be pleased to take you on." Thus speaking, Sanchez, six feet tall, 185 pounds, very muscular, very wiry, and swift as a cougar, removed his gunbelt and dismounted.

The gringos sheepishly put their weapons back in their holsters and just stood there for a moment, not knowing what move to make next. Meanwhile, Sanchez, quickly doing a series of loosening-up exercizes, for one tends to get a bit stiff from riding a horse or a mule for an extended period, then flexed his arm muscles and smiled at the gringos. Looking at big mouth, he said, "Ya know something, fatso, you look overfed and undernourished---your brain, that is, assuming that you have one!"

"Why, you dirty Mexican son of a buck," ol' big mouth said as he lunged toward Sanchez and took a wild swing.

Sanchez deftly stepped aside, then with a lightning movement grasped big mouth's arm, pulling it behind him and, taking advantage of the big fellow's momentum, sent him crashing into the rocks and brush just over the slope of the knoll, where he rolled two or three times before coming to a stop. Picking himself up and shaking his head to get his bearings, he bellered like a mad bull and made another lunge at Sanchez, this time apparently intending to overcome him with sheer weight and momentum. Sanchez, however, springy as a mountain lion and equally as fast, stepped aside and, snatching the big man's nose, lifted it half off his face.

Letting out a blood-curdling scream, the big fellow reached for his nose, which was bleeding profusely, the front of his shirt already drenched in blood. "You've pulled my nose part-way off, you rotten son of a buck!" he stammered, eyes wild as those of a cornered animal. You'll pay for this!"

Just then one of his partners drew a gun to shoot Sanchez, whose back was turned to him. A shot rang out, but it came from Julio's gun. The would-be assassin yelled with pain as he dropped his gun and, with his left hand, grabbed the injured arm to support it and to assuage the pain. The two other gringos had been in the act of drawing their weapons, but when Julio fired another round, they decided it would be wiser for them to leave good enough alone.

Sanchez, turning to Julio, said, "Keep 'em covered." Then to big mouth he said, "Well, fatso, have I made a believer out of you, or would you like some more abuse?" No answer. Quite drenched in blood, big mouth was tending to his nose. Then Sanchez, turning to the would-be assassin, who was still grasping his wounded arm, said, "You low-life scum, if it hadn't been for my friend here, you'd have shot me in the back, and then you worthless buzzards very likely would have murdered my two friends so they wouldn't be able to testify against you. The irony of this whole affair is that you brought it all onto yourselves. Surely you realize you're in **our** power now. If we had the same mind-set as you worthless bastards, we'd execute all four of you right here and now. This we're not going to do, but you **are** going to pay dearly for attacking us as you did. We're going to relieve you of all your clothes except your shirts. So strip everything off right now, underclothes and all. You two uninjured men help the other two off with their duds. Put your

50

money and other valuables in your shirt pockets or simply carry them in your hands."

Reluctantly the four obeyed as both Julio and Jose trained their pistols on them. "Now, if you have any matches," Sanchez told them, "you'd better take 'em along, for it's likely to turn chilly before you get home."

Once the four gringos were buck naked, Sanchez said, "Okay, fellas, put your shirts back on. The men complied, the two uninjured ones helping their compadres. "Now, which direction from here do you live?"

"West," one of them said.

"Fine," Sanchez countered, "you'll go east then. Now get moving. No, hold it. Put your hats on. Now get going, and pray most fervently that you never see us again. For if you do, we might not be so kindly disposed toward you would-be murderers. And, yes, one last thing---if your rear ends should get cold, check the foliage on the trees. Perhaps you might consider turning over a new leaf!"

What a grand sight they were, all four of them bare-assed and barefoot, tripping lightly down over the rocky knoll. Whether or not they were any wiser as a result of this self-induced confrontation would remain to be seen. . . .

After watching the four men disappear into the lily pads, Sanchez said, "Well, my friends, I am deeply indebted to you for saving my life. That was an unfortunate incident, and I probably didn't handle it with the utmost tact."

"On the contrary, Sanchez," Julio said, unable to suppress a smile. "You gave them ample opportunity to leave good enough alone, but their lack of judgment combined with their assumed superiority led to their humiliation. Forced humility is humility n'er forgotten, and I'll wager that those four will think carefully before running off at the mouth again."

"Imagine the wild story they'll concoct by the time they encounter anyone to relieve them of their plight!" Jose said laughing.

"Indeed," Sanchez agreed. "A regrettable and unfortunate incident though." Then glancing at the four horses, the camping equipment, the four rifles and eight pistols, he said, "Julio, maybe you could check their clothes for any extra ammunition, but remove only the ammunition, nothing else. And, Jose, why don't you help me to conceal these weapons in one of the packs? Let's leave their clothes lying right where they are---just in case the scoundrels decide to return and have a look around. Since the nights at this altitude are on the chilly side, we'll give them the benefit of the doubt by making their clothes available to them. As for their horses," he said addressing both men, "let's ride **them** and convert our three mules to pack animals. Since El Nino weighs over fifty pounds with the clay added, it will be a good idea to switch it from one animal to another every hour or so. . . ."

Progress toward Camarra was not only steady but somewhat accelerated after the untoward incident involving the four hunters. Sanchez had recommended that his party move closer to the Arizona border as they continued northward. "What do you think the chances are," he queried his companeros, "that big mouth and his friends will have turned back to see if we left their clothes at the campsite?"

"My guess," Julio said, "is that they will have done this because their home lies to the west anyway, and intuition might have prompted them to return to the campsite to see if any clothing or what could be adapted as such might still be there."

"You're echoing my thoughts exactly," Sanchez said. "And you, Jose, what would you say their next logical step would be?"

"Well," Jose began as if studying out what and how he was going to say it, "I'm worried that when those hombres get home they'll stir up a posse and come looking for us. And if they catch up with us before we make it to Camarra, we can expect some fireworks."

"My thoughts again," Sanchez said, "and this makes me regret my indiscretion of commenting that we had business dealings in Camarra. Course, at the time we had no way of knowing that our little confrontation would degenerate to the point that it did. What makes me feel worse is that I let emotion rather than prudence guide my responses to their questions. Looking back, one sees things more clearly!"

THE COMANCHES

About mid-afternoon three days later, with the peaks surrounding Camarra visible in the blue distance, the El Nino party was descending the slopes toward the valley floor. The sky was perfectly clear, the air cool, the only sounds those of their animals' hooves carefully negotiating the rocky terrain. Stopping momentarily to shift El Nino to one of the other pack horses, the men drank from their canteens and were just ready to get back on their horses when ominous sounds to their rear became audible, sounds of horses hooves and, moments later, the sounds of men's voices joining in.

"There the sons o' bucks are!" a raucus voice rang out.

"You're right," another voice yelled. "That's them all right."

At that point the voices, several of them joining in, were mostly indistinguishable except that it was clear that a shoot-out seemed imminent. "Quick!" Sanchez said. "Let's head for that stand of timber over there. Spread the horses out and tie each one to a tree. And, yes, we'll tie up the mule bearing El Nino. On second thought, let's take El Nino off the mule and hide it in the underbrush!"

No sooner had these plans been carried out till shots started to ring out, bullets richocheting on the surrounding rocks. "Julio," Sanchez said, "crawl over there to the right about thirty feet and position yourself down behind those bushes; and, Jose, run right over there to the left and position yourself behind that rock. I'll stay here behind this big pine." Each man had a high-powered rifle, two pistols, and ample ammunition.

"I saw the bastards headin right down through that draw!" a voice said excitedly. "Shoot the sons o' bucks on sight. Neither one of them bastards deserves to live! And, besides, those looked like our horses they wuz ridin."

As the members of the posse, ten men in all, headed down through the draw, weapons at the ready, three shots rang out and three posse members toppled from their horses. More shots followed, and one more posse member fell from his horse and rolled down among the rocks.

"Quick! Scatter out and dismount!" a voice called as additional shots rang out from the direction of Sanchez and friends, but the shots were not from **their** rifles. Others had joined in the fray.

"What in the hell's happening?" Sanchez said. "We must be surrounded. "Julio, you guard the rear till we can find out who's firing from that direction."

Shots continued to richochet from both east and west. A posse member suddenly let out a blood-curdling scream. "I'm hit! I'm hit!" he gasped as he fell headlong from behind a rock.

"Did you see that, Sanchez?" Jose exclaimed. "Somebody else's shootin at them fellers, and we're right in the middle of it."

"I know," Sanchez said. "Lie low."

More and more shots were being fired from the rear of Sanchez and party, hot lead richocheting and sparks flying from off the many rocks in the area. With the approach of whoever was providing the unexpected firepower, voices soon became audible. "Whoever they are," Sanchez said, "they're neither Mexican nor American. Those are Indians! How in tarnation did **they** get mixed up in this anyway?"

By this time the shooting from both the front and especially from the rear of Sanchez and party had intensified. "Why on earth," Sanchez said almost under his breath, "would Indians be helping us? There's never been too much love lost between these Norteamericano Indians, whether Comanches, Apaches, or whoever and the Mexicans. So why would they be helping us?"

As the bullets kept flying, an Indian not more than about thirty or forty feet from Sanchez and party screamed in pain, then dropped to the ground. A cacophony of voices could be heard from both the front and the rear of the Mexicans. Then suddenly two more posse members sounded their death knell as they fell over, both mortally wounded.

"Let's git the hell outa here!" a desperate-sounding posse member said. "We rode right into a hornet's nest." A mad scramble ensued as the remaining three posse members tried to get on their horses, but no sooner had two of them swung part-way into their saddles when they fell to the ground to breathe their last. Only one man of the original ten posse members managed to get away, and he went zigzagging up through the timber to safety.

Meanwhile, the Indians, advancing steadily, suddenly saw Sanchez and Julio. "Don't shoot! Don't shoot!" Sanchez called out in English while dropping his weapon and putting his hands in the air. It was a split-second kind of decision, for he was unaware of whether the Indians had known that he and his two partners had also been shooting at the posse members.

"Who the hell are you!" one of the Indians called out. "How'd you guys git into this fight? Whose side are you on anyway? Were you shooting at those bastards or at us?"

"At them!" Sanchez said.

"At them?!" the Indian said. "Why in the hell would you fellers be shootin at them when they were government agents out to arrest us?"

"They were shooting at **us**, not at you guys!" Sanchez explained.

"The hell they weren't shooting at us," the Indian said. "We were camped right down there," he said pointing, "when all of a sudden bullets started crashing in among us, killing one of our men outright. And you can sit there and say they weren't shooting at us?" By now he was joined by more than a dozen of his group. "Them bastards from the government have been following us for about two weeks and finally caught up with us."

"I'm sorry to have to contradict you, my friend," Sanchez said, "but those were members of a posse out looking for us."

"Out looking for **you**?" the Indian asked in disbelief. "How do you know them fellers wasn't government agents?"

"Well, that's quite simple. You see, several days ago we had a run-in with four white hunters, all smart asses who first insulted us and then tried to kill us. Without boring you with the specific details, we managed to get the better of them and sent them away on foot with only their shirts and hats."

"You're bullshittin us!" the Indian said. "Why in the hell would you send them away without their clothes?"

"We wanted to teach the impudent bastards a lesson. They'd have shot me in the back if one of my two friends here hadn't shot the one in the arm just as he was ready to fire his pistol at me. Anyway, we told them to keep their money and other valuables and to take off down the hill wearing only their shirts and hats!"

"That sounds like a cock and bull story if I've ever heard one before," the Indian said, "but it's funny as hell!" And with that he and his partners laughed heartily.

"I admit that it's a bizarre situation," Sanchez said smiling, "but it happened exactly as I've explained it. Then just awhile ago when the posse members spotted us, they yelled out, 'That's them! Them's the bastards that took our clothes, our guns, and our horses. Shoot 'em. Neither one of them Mexican bastards deserves to live after what they did to us!' And then they headed down into this little draw firing at anything that moved. We quickly dismounted and hid our horses nearby and took up our positions. They were spraying the whole area with rifle and pistol fire when right off the bat we shot three of them. Then shortly after that we were startled when we heard shots being fired from behind us, and especially when we saw a number of posse members mortally wounded. 'Who on earth would be helping us?' I asked my two friends. Then as you gentlemen got closer we could hear you talking to one another; and since you were speaking neither Spanish nor English, we concluded that you must be Indians. But, needless to say, we were completely baffled as to why Indians would be helping **us**! 'How,' we asked ourselves, 'would Indians even know who we were or who the posse members were?'"

"Well, I'll be a son of a buck," the Indian said smiling. Then turning to some of his men who had just returned from inspecting the dead posse members and to relieve them of their guns and ammunition and other valuables, he said, "Looks like we did okay with all them weapons. Did you git their ammunition and money and hunting knives and pocketknives, too?"

"Yes, Beno," one of them said. "Everything's right here. The two shots you just heard was to kill two of their badly wounded horses."

"I thought so," their leader said. "I knew you was either finishing off some horses or men or both. Was all of the men

56

dead? You know we can't leave any evidence indicating that we had anything to do with that bunch."

"All of the men appeared to be dead as doornails, but we did have to finish off the two horses. We took the bridles and saddles off first, then shot the poor creatures to get them out of their misery; they'd been wounded bad in the crossfire. So we ended up with all these weapons and seven horses and two extra bridles and saddles and some knives. Not bad, huh, Beno?"

"Not bad at all, Thomas," Beno said grinning. "Not bad at all." Then turning to Sanchez, he said, "So now, what exactly brings you fellers all the way up here in this part of the country anyway?"

"We'd been invited to come up and work for a few months in the silver mine over by Camarra," Sanchez volunteered. "It was an offer we couldn't refuse. Course, we also had another object in coming. One of our friends there at the mine had his mule and a little pack burro stolen, so we are bringing him a replacement, which he'll greatly appreciate. As you know, a man's pretty much hamstrung without transportation, especially when he urgently needs it; and, of course, one never knows when he will have a pressing need for reliable transportation."

"Quite true," Beno said. "So this then is the sum and substance of your errand? You're not hiding anything from us?"

"This is it, my Friend," Sanchez said smiling. "I refer to you as Friend' because you and your men came to our assistance. We were outnumbered ten to three; course, right off the bat we sent three of them to the happy hunting grounds! "

"And what about the big fellow up there with the bandaged nose?" one of the braves asked.

"Oh, him!" Sanchez said. "Well, you see, he was the big mouth that started the whole thing. We gave them several chances to leave good enough alone and to let us go on about our business, but the big fellow, egged on by his compadres, kept agitating and then finally insulting us till I challenged them to put their weapons away and to take me on one at a time or even two at a time for that matter. So big mouth, thinking he could bully me with his sheer weight and size, came at me as if he'd gone completely loco. Things turned out badly for him; and then

57

as I was facing away from his partners for a moment, one of 'em pulled a gun on me and was about to shoot me in the back, but my friend Julio shot him in the right arm, causing him to drop the weapon. From that point on, things degenerated for the impudent bastards, and to teach them a lasting lesson we sent them away with just their shirts and hats."

Beno and company laughed heartily at this. "That's one helluva story, feller. It sounds like it might be true. But even if it isn't, you're one helluva storyteller anyway."

"As I said," Sanchez continued, "that posse was out for blood; and when they spotted us heading down through this little draw, they started spraying the whole area with bullets, and you gentlemen happened to be right in their line of fire. We deeply regret that one of your men was killed by them. You were unaware of us and them, and they were unaware of you as we likewise were unaware of you until you men started shooting. A strange set of circumstances any way you want to look at it!" Sanchez added with a smile.

All of the Indians, Comanches as it turned out, seemed intrigued by what Sanchez had to say. His two partners seemed to get the drift of the conversation although they didn't speak any English. Most of the Indians, however, appeared to understand what was being said.

Naturally curious about what these Comanches were up to, Sanchez said, "If I may ask, why are you gentlemen being pursued by government agents?"

"Mainly for leaving the reservation," Beno said. He seemed to be in charge of their enterprise, whatever it was exactly. "The government," he continued, "has an absolute knack for creating reservations out of the most undesirable land around, and we quite frankly are fed up with it. We're supposed to farm the land, but there's so little water that crops don't amount to anything. And on top of that, the hunting in the mountains isn't anything to crow about either. We're just fed up with conditions in general. This whole big country belonged to the Indians till the white man arrived and proceeded to push the Indians around. Their attitude from the very first was that the Indians were nothing but savages, not real human beings. Consequently, the Indians have been pushed and shoved off their land until there isn't anywhere else to go. As for us, well, we raised a bit of hell on the reservation and either had to leave for a while or go to jail; as you can see, we opted to leave and have been on the run from the law ever since. That's why we thought we were being attacked by government agents when all the shooting started, especially when one of our men got it right through the heart."

"That's a sad circumstance indeed," Sanchez said, "and we're sorry for this misfortune. It seems like a freakish thing that your man could have been shot by a stray bullet, and right through the heart at that."

"Fortunately, he is not married like most of us, so he won't be leaving a wife and children behind, but his family members will grieve over him. . . ."

"I must comment on your excellent command of the language," Sanchez said after a somewhat awkward pause. "How is it that you speak English so well?"

"That's quite simple," Beno said smiling, obviously pleased with the compliment. "I'm a teacher at the reservation. I graduated from the University of Arizona, where I was looked upon more or less as a seven-days' wonder since it was most unusual for an Indian to have advanced far enough with his education to enroll at a university. The fact that I got good grades made me even more of an anomaly. I majored in English and minored in teaching. Now, I don't always speak as correctly as I know how, but I assure you that I do know the difference and can speak the King's English if I have to. All of which leads me to ask you a similar question. How is it that you, a Mexican, speak English without a trace of an accent? This I find most unusual because most native speakers of Spanish, at least those I've spoken with, rarely ever learn to speak English without belying their linguistic background."

"First off, I appreciate your kind words about my facility with English. I spent over two years working in Columbus, New Mexico, where I immersed myself in the English language; and, thanks to a wonderful tutor who drilled me hour after hour, I somehow managed to lose my accent. I make no effort to hide the fact that I take a certain amount of pleasure in this achievement, and besides speaking English every time the opportunity presents itself, I also read voraciously. For instance, I've read most of Shakespeare's thirty-seven plays and all of his sonnets."

"Shall I compare thee to a summer's day? Thou art more lovely and more temperate," Beno said laughing. "'Tis clear that you're another seven-days' wonder." Both men laughed while the others merely looked puzzled.

"Sonnet 18," Sanchez said proudly. "I'm impressed. . . . Anyway, part of the anticipated pleasure I derive from this little excursion into the United States is being able to speak English since most of the people working at the mine in Camarra are Americans."

While this conversation was in progress, a number of the braves had been sizing up the horses, mules, and burros belonging to Sanchez and party. One of the men, stumbling upon El Nino, came running up to their leader. "Beno," he said somewhat excitedly, "we've just come across a strange object right over there in that bush. It's quite heavy, and we have no idea what it is."

"Oh, that!" Sanchez said, trying to play it cool. "That represents an additional facet of our errand in Camarra. As a gift from our people in Ascension to the parish in Camarra, we are transporting a painted plaster of paris statue of El Nino, which is Spanish for the Christ Child. Since plaster of paris, as you know, is very fragile, we were advised to pack the statue in clay so it would not be broken if the pack animal transporting it should have an accident, such as stumbling and falling down or the like. In consideration to our pack animals, we've been switching the statue from one animal to the other every hour or so."

Beno and company immediately started over to have a look at the object, which was encased by a wooden covering and encircled by several strands of baling wire for additional security. Sizing it up from all angles, the Comanche leader turned to Sanchez. "You wouldn't be bullshittin us about the contents of this crate, would you?"

"Certainly not," Sanchez said. "This was the only conceivable way to pack the statue to secure it from breakage, for if it should be broken, then our whole endeavor would be blasted, leaving us with some hefty explaining when we get back to Ascension."

"You could be carrying something of far greater value than a plaster-of-paris statue," the Comanche said, grinning maliciously. "Would it upset you if we had a look?"

"My Friend," Sanchez said, still playing it cool, "that's an odd question. Let me give you a candid answer. Course, it would upset me, for to remove the clay from the statue requires some uncommon expertise. The least false move would shatter the statue, and that naturally speaks for itself. If I may be so bold, why is it that you are so curious about this crate? Surely you wouldn't expect three poor Mexicans like us to be carrying anything of great monetary value, would you? Our sole motive, no more and no less, is to present this beautifully sculpted statue of El Nino to our sister parish in Camarra. We're of the opinion that exchanges such as this not only between people of like religions but between people of different countries can do a great deal to foster international understanding and good will. It is with these humanitarian ideals in mind that we have transported this statue these 150 or so miles over some very rough and forbidding terrain. How utterly disappointing it would be for us and also for the proposed recipients of this gift if now, with Camarra itself within view, we should have an accident and damage the statue."

Listening intently but with a malicious gleam in his eyes, the Comanche said, "Amigo, as I noted earlier, you're a consummate storyteller. What you've been saying could be true, and at the same time it could be false; and, frankly, you have me in somewhat of a quandary. I don't know whether I should believe you, for if the crate contains something very valuable such as silver, gold, or platinum, we're very interested. We'd like to have a look. I realize that to violate the---should I say---sanctity of whatever is in this crate would be regarded by most folks as ungentlemanly, unkind, unfair, unethical, and all of that business. But, you see, my people---the American Indians in general---have been treated so unfairly over the years that I occasionally seek to justify my skullduggery as a means of getting even in various and sundry ways."

"Your words fall upon sympathetic ears, my Friend," Sanchez said, still calm and self-assured. "But perhaps you're not thinking about the incontrovertible fact that the Americans literally seized a mammoth chunk of Mexico and annexed it to the United States. We happen to be standing right now on part of that expropriated territory. So you see, we Mexicans have been disenfranchised by the white Americans just the same as you native peoples have. Should not that fact alone provide sufficient impetus for us to respect one another's rights? The farthest thing from our minds is to take advantage of you gentlemen or of anyone else for that matter. As a boy growing up, I was taught about the sanctity of each individual. My parents impressed this important principle upon me and my brothers and sisters during our weekly devotionals in the home; and then, of course, we received the same teachings in church. Christianity in action, our priest told us, adding that when people everywhere decide to live in accordance with this principle, then peace will prevail throughout the Earth."

"Paul," the Comanche said half laughing, "almost thou makest a believer out of me!"

"Would that I might make a believer not only out of thee but of thy entire household!" Sanchez said.

"You're no fool, Amigo," the Comanche said smiling, "and I'm not either. I can't explain it exactly, but something about your story doesn't ring true. And to be right frank with you, I believe you're transporting something very valuable inside that crate, whether it be a statue or whatever. I am inclined to ask you to open it for inspection."

"But, my Friend," Sanchez countered, "you're asking the wrong person. The expert who does this sort of thing resides in Camarra. I'd be pleased to satisfy your curiosity if I had the skills required to remove the clay from this statue. Better yet, I suggest that you gentlemen accompany us to Camarra so you can watch the entire process of removing the clay from El Nino, as people fondly refer to this statue."

"Amigo, you're hedging again," the Comanche said. "I'd wager any two of these horses that the crate contains a precious metal of one kind or another, with you gentlemen being nothing more and nothing less than curriers of the same. At this point you've turned me into a modern version of Pandora, whose curiosity finally got her so stirred up that she no longer could resist the temptation to open the famed box."

"Quite true, my Friend," Sanchez replied, "but surely you haven't forgotten that when earth's first mortal woman broke the seal on the box its lid flew open, releasing all of the plagues that since have tormented mankind. Are you willing to risk something similar for yourself and your men?"

"Amigo, the question of opening this crate for inspection has just taken a new twist. Now you're intimating that something drastic will happen if we open the crate or attempt to open it!"

At this point one of the braves, having grown impatient with this verbal jousting, pulled out his revolver and fired what he had intended to be a glancing shot to break the wire strands securing the crate. He and his partners were in for a big surprise, however, for when he pulled the trigger his revolver blew up in his hand, badly injuring the same and causing him to howl with pain. The crate remained unscathed.

Immediately picking up on this incident, Sanchez told the Comanche, "You see, my Friend, you in effect are treading on holy ground; you're not supposed to violate the sanctity of this crate, for the object contained therein is sacred. You've just been given a sign. If I might be so bold to say so, I wouldn't press the issue any further. The results could be disastrous."

"Good try, Amigo," the Comanche said with a chuckle. "This is merely an isolated incident. I frankly don't believe it was the result of any kind of supernatural intervention, which you were quick to pick up on, thinking---as to be expected---that all native people are naturally superstitious."

"You, of course, are entitled to your opinion, my Friend, but in all candor I must say that it will be counter-productive if you make any further attempts to open this crate."

"Come now, Amigo," the Comanche said laughing. "That's just so much bullshit. You're trying to drown us in blather. "

Then turning to one of his men standing nearby, he said, "Bunko, you have a sharp pocketknife. See if you can cut these wires."

With noticeable reluctance Bunko stepped forward and, inspecting his pocketknife, selected the blade he thought would do the job. But as soon as he touched the first wire on the crate, a monstruous and highly explosive spark enveloped him as several hundred volts knocked him ass over teakettle and rolled him several times till he collided with a tree. Most of the other braves gasped as they fell all over one another trying to get thirty or forty feet away to hide behind the closest tree or rock.

"Did I not tell you, my Friend?" Sanchez said calmly though not accusingly to the Comanche.

"Look, Amigo," the latter said, "I don't scare easily. I actually believe that you are some kind of charlatan and that you yourself cleverly engineered this whole thing."

"I most sincerely thank you for the left-handed compliment, my Friend," Sanchez said, "but, alas, I personally can't take any credit for what just happened. At the very most I was simply the conduit, if you will, through whom the information was channeled to you. A Higher Power is telling you not to violate the sanctity of the statue contained in this crate. The statue represents the Christ Child; and when looking directly into the eyes of El Nino, people report that it must not be much different from looking into the very eyes of Christ Himself. I have had this experience, and I can tell you unabashedly that this is true. You indeed are playing with fire, very hot fire in this case, and if I were you I'd calmly and wisely back away from this situation."

"Amigo," the Comanche said, "when given the chance I'll recommend that you be elected to the U. S. Congress, for when it comes to filibustering, you have no peers. Your reasoning, admittedly, is logical, but I myself am an out and out pragmatist. I don't believe in the supernatural even though I sometimes go along with the antics of my compatriots here just to maintain my position of leadership among them. They're satisfied with this, for reasoning things out logically and coolly is not one of their virtues. They prefer superstition and the unexplainable. Myself, I believe in cause and effect.

"My Friend," Sanchez said, "I am trying to prevent you from rushing headlong into disaster. But like lemmings rushing en masse into the sea, you seem overly intent on turning yourself into a piece of burned toast."

Laughing, the Comanche said, "Amigo, in your overt concern for my welfare you just did a great job mixing a simile and a metaphor!"

"Yes, I realized the same as soon as the words left my mouth; but aside from literary style, I am most concerned for you. In fact, since you refuse to be dissuaded from your dangerous enterprise, let me have you try a little experiment. Hold your hands about six or eight inches away from the crate and see if you don't feel a strange heat emanating from it."

"You're trying to make me look foolish in front of my men, Amigo!"

"Not at all. I merely want you to see that you're dealing with a sacred object, which to violate will have dire consequences."

"All right. I'll do it to satisfy you, to show you that there really is nothing to all this hokus-pokus business you've been subjecting us to." And with that the Comanche held both hands close to the crate and then suddenly withdrew them. Then he again held out his hands, almost touching the crate and again withdrew them.

"So what did I tell you, my Friend? Now you've seen for yourself that I'm not just talking through my teeth. Twice you felt a strange heat coming from the crate, didn't you?"

"Yes, I did, Amigo. But I'm still not convinced. I think you're tricking us. You have an ace of some kind up your sleeve."

"If you really think so, my friend, then why don't you actually touch the crate? Show your men what a brave Brave you are! I dare you!"

Hesitating for a moment, the Comanche said, "All right. I'll do it, and I'll prove to you that nothing drastic will happen." All of his men had been listening intently to this unusual verbal exchange, and now they edged forward slightly to see what might happen if their leader touched the crate. Hesitantly he reached down and, almost touching the crate, withdrew his hands.

"Go on, my Friend," Sanchez told him. "Let's see a little display of your machismo. Make yourself look good in the eyes of your compadres here. After all, you just got through stating that superstition means nothing to you. So go ahead and prove it!"

Again the Comanche bent down to touch the crate, edging ever closer until his hands actually touched it. Strangely warm it was, but nothing beyond that happened. His confidence now increasing, he then put both hands squarely on the crate; and since nothing out of the ordinary happened, he slapped the sides of the crate a couple times, then turned triumphantly to Sanchez. "See, Amigo," he said laughing, but none too confidently, "I did it, which proves that your wizardry doesn't always work."

Undeterred by this seeming setback, Sanchez countered with, "For the time being perhaps. You see, I'm not the one in control of El Nino. I've seen far too much from this statue to place undue confidence in your handling of it with impunity. For instance, I've seen literally hundreds of sick and afflicted folks healed by merely looking at this statue of El Nino and exercising their faith in its beneficent powers. I also saw a big macho man, a follower of Pancho Villa, drop totally out of sight for reaching up and slapping El Nino on both sides of the face. And being a party to this, Villa and the men with him scattered like rabbits."

"My Friend," the Comanche said with an 'I told you I could do it' look, "you just saw what I did, and sbsolutely nothing happened."

"But you have no assurance whatsoever that nothing yet will happen! Can you say with any certainty whatsoever that one of these first nights you'll awaken with your guts on fire and have no way to extinguish the blaze?"

"You're a real die-hard, aren't you, Amigo?"

"Perhaps so, but above all I'm a realist; and my unsolicited advice to you, my Friend, is DON'T MAKE LIGHT OF SACRED THINGS."

"Amigo, whatever there is of a sacred nature about this crate and its supposed contents is all a figment of your imagination. You were leading us down the equivalent of a primrose path, but now we've emerged into the light of day. I say there's nothing to this baloney about a sacred object or statue, whatever it's alleged to be, inside this crate. I say that it contains precious metal of some kind, and sooner or later I'm going to find out."

"My Friend," Sanchez retorted philosophically, "if you do, it will be with the most serious of consequences. Remember that I have warned you."

"That you have. Indeed you have." This said, the Comanche turned to his men and, addressing them in their native dialect, told them to point their loaded weapons at Sanchez and his two compadres.

"My friend," Sanchez said in amazement, "what on earth are you doing? Why are your men pointing their weapons at us?"

"Amigo," the Comanche said laughing, "a fascinating thought has just crossed my mind. I, as leader of this Comanche band, will deliver this package to the church in Camarra, which means that as of now you and your two helpers are relieved of this responsibility. As for your alleged intentions of working in the silver mine near Camarra, that was merely a ruse to cover up your real intention, which was to deliver this crate of precious metal and then to walk away with loads of money jingling in your pockets."

"Surely, my Friend," Sanchez countered, "you can't be serious. What a fertile imagination you have!"

"And this is not all, Amigo," the Comanche said. "You see, since we will be delivering the statue or whatever is in the crate, you no longer will have need of your horses and pack mules. Unlike you in your treatment of the white hunters, we'll not require you to leave here naked, but you will leave here empty-handed, for as of now everything you have, except your clothes of course, is ours." Then turning to his men, he said, "Relieve them of their weapons and ammunition." This done, he said exultantly, "This has been a good day. Just look at all of the horses, weapons, and ammunition we now have. And, above all, whatever is in that crate is also ours!" Again turning to Sanchez

67

and party, he crowed, "Amigos, to be truthful, I must admit that there never was much love lost between Comanches and Mexicans! Now I'm afraid it is time for you gentlemen to hit the trail---the trail whence you came. At least you'll be leaving with all your clothes. . . ."

Wisdom dictating that Sanchez say no more, he motioned for his two compadres to follow, and they proceeded at once to retrace their steps.

SWEET REVENGE

To see that the three Mexicans were serious about hitting the trail, the Comanche leader told his braves to fire a number of rounds near them, which they did, some of the bullets hitting dangerously close and ricocheting in all directions. This, of course, had the desired effect, for the Mexicans hastily made tracks and were soon out of sight. But that's as far as they went. "We'll wait here, compadres," Sanchez told them, "to keep an eye on that bunch. The final chapter of this episode has not been written."

Meantime, while some of the Comanches were rounding up the horses, mules, and burros, the rest, following their leader's instructions, proceeded to place El Nino into a pack on one of the burros. This accomplished, their leader said, "Men, we too must hit the trail, but it won't be to Camarra. We'll head due north toward the Four Corners country, which will give us sufficient time to figure out just what we're going to do with this crate of whatever it is. Let's not waste time now, however, in trying to find out what's in it." This said, they began their move northward, but because of the additional animals now in their keep, they were unable to move as fast as they normally would have.

Sanchez, Julio, and Jose, careful to stay out of sight, followed closely, for all three were rugged men and no strangers to hard physical labor. Hence, they had little difficulty keeping up with the Indians. The latter proceeded northward until after sundown, then stopped to camp for the night, certain that no one was aware of them or their nefarious activities.

But unbeknown to the Comanches, men other than Sanchez and party would soon become involved in these bizarre happenings. For instance, the lone posse member who had managed to escape had ridden like the wind until reaching his home in Eagle Bluff, quickly spreading the news of the massacre. As to be expected, the entire town was up in arms and out for blood, the blood of three Mexicans and fifteen or so Comanches. Moreover, the local sheriff had had presence of mind to alert other law officers at strategic points north, including Camarra, although he was reasonably sure that neither the Mexicans nor the Indians would be shortsighted enough to stop there.

As darkness came, the Comanches finished eating their supper and then, bellies full, proceeded to become quite boisterous about their phenomenal exploits of the day. They lavished praise upon their fearless leader, for he had outsmarted the silver-tongued Mexican. What's more, in a day or two after they had had time to think through the situation, they would open the crate to see exactly what it contained. And if their hunch was right, for they were encouraged by their leader in this, the crate very likely would contain precious metal of one kind or another, silver or gold or the like, and this would mean that all of them could end up rich.

After an hour or so of reveling in their cleverness, first one and then another proceeded to find a comfortable spot to curl up in his blanket and get some much-needed rest. A guard was posted to keep an eye on the animals, all of which had been staked out in a little grassy meadow nearby so they could crop grass and rest intermittently during the night. The Indians saw no need to relieve the animals of their packs or their saddles during the night. "Why bother?" they had concluded. After all, if it should become necessary to make a hasty departure, they'd lose no time fiddling around with packs and saddles.

It being a moonless night, Sanchez, Julio, and Jose had to be especially careful as they crept ever closer to the Indian encampment. Nothing more than a snapping twig could reveal their presence. Soon they were close enough to observe the guard's every move. The three Mexicans, crouching behind trees, waited for the right opportunity to make their move. Before long the guard, tired like his partners and fully confident that no one had followed them, began to doze from time to time and soon was snoring contentedly. Stealthily as a cat, Sanchez, martial arts expert that he was, approached the sleeping Comanche and, with one deft, silent movement, broke his neck. Removing the ammunition from his pockets and taking his rifle, he motioned for his partners to follow. Quietly they walked out

70

among the horses so as not to spook them and singled out the three they had been riding. Then they carefully led the horses, the two mules, and the burros to the opposite end of the meadow and far enough into the timber to be out of sight.

"Let's open Susie's pack," Sanchez said, Susie being the one little burro that carried the guns they had confiscated from the four white hunters. "Come daylight there's gonna be one helluva showdown between three Mexicans and about fourteen Comanches." They were greatly disappointed, however, to discover that El Nino was in neither of the packs. The Comanches apparently had removed the crate and concealed it in the bushes next to their encampment. "Well," Sanchez mused, "it looks as if we'll have to wait till morning to retrieve El Nino. But we will. No more playing nice guys to these underhanded yahoos."

Long about 4 a.m. a terrible moaning and groaning could be heard among the Comanches. Listening carefully, Sanchez said, "That's their leader's voice. He's obviously in great pain. I warned El Jerko about what he could expect if he insisted on stealing the statue from us."

The moaning and groaning persisted and presently erupted into loud, pitiful wails. "Oh, my guts are on fire!" the Comanche leader howled in English while holding his stomach and stumbling around the remains of their campfire. "My guts are on fire! My guts are on fire! Water! Water! Who the hell's got some water? Oh, my insides are being fried! Oh! Oh! Oh! I'm being cooked alive! Somebody help me! Help me, somebody!"

The entire encampment was awake by now, and two or three of the braves fetched water for their tormented leader, who quickly gulped it down, but it failed to quench the fire in his innards. "My guts!" he moaned. "My guts! They're on fire! I'm being burned alive from the inside out!"

Just then an excited brave came running from the edge of the meadow shouting, "Three Feathers is dead! Three Feathers is dead, and his rifle's missing!" This news, added to their leader's dilemma, caused near pandemonium in the encampment.

"Go check the horses!" someone called out, and a couple braves ran into the meadow, only to return with the news that

71

three horses and four pack animals were missing. Meanwhile, one of the braves had put some wood on the dying embers, causing the area around the ailing leader to light up. "Oh, my guts are burning!" the tormented Indian wailed. "I'm being burned alive from the inside out!"

Just then a rifle shot pierced the air, and the Comanche leader fell headlong into the fire to breathe his last. Indians scattered in all directions, each one's weapon lying next to a deserted blanket.

"That'll teach the impudent bastards how the cow eats the cabbage," Sanchez said. "They had more than ample warning but chose to ignore it."

By now it was beginning to get light. "Let the first son of a buck of 'em show his face," Sanchez said, "and he's the same as a dead Injun. Presently two of the braves could be seen creeping back very carefully to pick up their weapons. "Julio," Sanchez whispered, "on the count of three, you plug the one on the left and I'll get the one on the right. One, two, three!" Two shots rang out simultaneously, and two braves dropped to the ground, never to rise again. "I regret to have to say it," Sanchez told his partners, "but as long as any of 'em are still alive, the three of us are in trouble." Minutes later a single brave could be seen crawling toward his weapon. "This one's yours, Jose," Sanchez whispered. Taking careful aim, Jose plugged him right between the eyes.

No one stirred around the Indian encampment for the next hour. "Either they're waiting until they think the coast is clear, or they don't plan to return for their weapons. We'll wait a while longer to see what happens. Meantime, my Friends," Sanchez continued, "we're on the horns of a dilemma. It's a sure cinch that the lone posse member who got away yesterday will have alerted the law and that by now it is quite likely that lawmen all up along the line are either converging or getting ready to converge on the approximate area north of here where they would expect us to go. Moreover, our important errand will be nullified if we don't figure out a way to get over to the Indian encampment to find El Nino. My guess is that the statue is only feet away from where they were eating. What do you guys think our options are at this point?"

"Well, I'll tell you, Sanchez," Jose began. "The situation looks grim at the moment, but I think we can still retrieve El Nino. In fact, if you fellers will keep me covered, I'll slip around the edge of this little meadow and see what I can find out."

"How does that sound to you, Julio?" Sanchez asked. "Do we dare let Jose give it a try?"

"Jose's no fool," Julio said. "He's naturally cautious, so I believe we should let him try it."

"Okay, Amigo," Sanchez said. "But be very careful, and we'll do our level best to keep you covered if we detect the least movement in and around the encampment. When you get over to the south end of the meadow, step to the edge of the clearing and wave to us so we'll know precisely where you are."

Rifle in hand and gunbelt strapped around his waist, Jose, well concealed by the surrounding trees, headed around to the south end of the meadow. Minutes later he waved. Sanchez and Julio, rifles at the ready, surveyed with eagle eyes the area around the encampment but could detect no movement.

Suddenly a shot rang out, followed by a death knell. Then, to their relief, they saw Jose waving and indicating that they should fire a few shots into the area immediately behind the encampment. So they in turn fired several well-placed shots into the trees, and by sheer luck one of the bullets found its mark, for another brave screamed, followed by some mad scrambling by several men retreating back into the trees as fast as they could move. Jose, edging closer to the burned-out fire, soon spotted the crate containing El Nino and communicated the same by hand signals to his two partners. Then he motioned for one of them to lead Susie around through the trees so they could put the crate into one of her packbags. During the interim Jose carefully surveyed his immediate surroundings to see if he might detect any movement. He saw none, concluding that the braves apparently had retreated further into the trees since in their haste they had left their weapons next to their blankets.

73

Presently Julio appeared with Susie, and in little time he and Jose had loaded the crate in one of her packbags. Into the other packbag they placed all of the rifles they could find, then returned whence they'd come, Jose, rifle in hand, walking backward just in case one of the braves should take a shot at them. Horses were scattered all over the meadow, some of them cropping grass and a few of them too nervous to eat.

"Excellent work, Amigos," Sanchez said smiling. "Since heading for the cave just north of Camarra is totally out of the question, it seems to me that we should bear off to the northeast before heading due north again. How does this plan strike you guys?"

"Sounds fine to me," Julio said. "We're probably in trouble either way we go, but my guess is that to head northeast is our best option."

"I'm with you in this decision," Jose said.

"From a purely practical standpoint," Sanchez volunteered, "I suppose we could bury El Nino around here somewhere, but the disadvantage in doing this is that if we should be killed, no one would know where to look for El Nino."

"If you recall, we've spoken a number of times," Jose said thoughtfully, "about those big caves up north of Four Corners. Padre de Escalante even mentioned one of them as an option."

"He did. I well recall him suggesting it as a secondary possibility," Julio said. "But he didn't dwell on it, apparently because he seemed particularly confident that we'd reach the sacred cave just north of Camarra. This is a difficult option since it's a helluva long way up there. Our present situation lends new meaning to the expression 'between a rock and a hard place.'"

"You, unfortunately, are right about that," Sanchez said, smiling wanly. "And that route, it goes without saying, is fraught with difficulties, not just in terms of rugged terrain and determined lawmen but also in terms of Navajos, who are all over that country and probably know every little nook and cranny for a few hundred miles in every direction. That they would be aware of the caves up on what they call Grand Bench is a given, so if we do make it up there, we'll have to be

74

particularly ingenious in hiding El Nino so that no one will find it. Then when the coast is finally clear, we can return for it."

"Tell me, Sanchez," Julio began philosophically, "I know this might turn out to be an inane question, but why did we not bury El Nino right close to Ascension, perhaps at a certain spot in the surrounding hills?"

"Good question, Amigo," Sanchez stated. "I myself put that same question to Padre de Escalante, who said that it has something to do with a prophecy about great riches in monetary wealth along with even greater riches in terms of the increased numbers of healings that will occur when El Nino returns from the sacred cave north of Camarra to grace once more the Cathedral of the Blessed Virgin. If it truly is God's will that we hide the statue either in that cave or in one of the caves up on Grand Bench, then I suppose all human judgment is automatically eliminated from the decision. God's ways are not man's ways, as the prophet says. Surely the LORD knew of any number of better places than the Sinai Peninsula for the ancient Israelites' forty-year sojourn, but He had His reasons for keeping those rebellious souls there, the older ones in particular. Anyway, I suppose we simply have to take on faith the notion that our present goal is Grand Bench, which if you perchance have taken a look at a map of that area is on the southeast side of the Kaiparowits Plateau. To get there will necessitate our crossing the Colorado River, probably at Lee's Ferry. If it weren't for the highly risky business of having to transport El Nino across the river, we simply could swim our animals across while holding onto their tails. This, I understand, is an old trick long perfected by the Navajos. Our pretext for venturing up into those parts can be the phenomenal hard-coal deposits there in the Buckskin Mountains, through which we will have to travel to get to Grand Bench. Literally millions of junipers dot that lonely landscape, and if it weren't for the mountains---or so I've been told---one could get lost quite easily. But the higher peaks in the area provide some wonderful reference points."

Glancing at Jose and grinning, Julio said with a sigh, "Well, that at least clears up a number of questions that have been bouncing around in my mind. It doesn't simplify things much;

75

but, if nothing more, it does give us a fair idea of what's in store for us."

"It's also going to be a supreme test of our faith and endurance," Jose added. "But we've all been a party to some of the wondrous things brought to pass by El Nino; and since we have the specific assignment of depositing the statue temporarily in one of those caves, we must be confident that God somehow will open up the way for us to accomplish what we've been commissioned to do."

"Impressively stated, Jose," Sanchez said. "Your confidence and positive attitude are good for me to hear, for what lies ahead is not kids' play by any stretch of the imagination. . . ."

ENTER THE LAW

"McClanahan," Sheriff Anderson over in Eagle Bluff said familiarly to his chief deputy, "have you taken a close look at every man's outfit to see if we're ready to move out?"

"That I have, sheriff," his right-hand man said proudly as his Adam's apple moved up and down quite noticeably. "I looked at bedrolls, grub, and weapons, and everyone appears to be waiting for your command to hit the trail. Oh, yes, and all of the horses have been shod."

"Good man," the sheriff said. "Gentlemen, first off I want to express my appreciation for the wonderful response from all of you to drop whatever it wuz you wuz a doin to join with us in this worthy undertakin. As you know, we've lost nine of our best men these past few days; and the scoundrels that did it, whether they be Mexicans, Indians, or whoever, are gonna feel the long arm of the law. In simpler language that means that some of 'em very likely are gonna feel what it's like to have a noose around their necks---that is, of course, if the law finds 'em guilty. Anyway, without further ado, let's head for the foothills, which we'll follow till we git up to Camarra." The troops now moving, the sheriff, speaking loud enough for everyone to hear and looking around at his posse members, said, "At that point we'll be joinin forces with my good friend Sheriff Lawson, and some of us very likely will stick to the foothills while Lawson's men head up into the mountains. It's my understanding that Sheriff Bronson and his men up in Stevensville are already scouring the nearby mountains and questioning anyone they happen upon."

Just east of Camarra, Sheriff Lawson and his men hit paydirt, so to speak, by the time they had arrived in the foothills east of town. Seven or eight Comanches, all on horseback and without weapons, were heading down out of the hills toward town to explain their plight to the sheriff. Seeing the Comanches approach, the sheriff called out, "Men, have your weapons ready, but for hell's sake don't shoot unless I give the command. Let's see what these fellers have to say."

The Comanche spokesman, whose command of English left a great deal to be desired, said, "Sheriff, we 'tacked by big bunch Mexicans. They shoot bang, bang, bang and kill us. Don't know why Mexicans shoot Indians."

Looking at the rest of the Comanches, the sheriff asked, "Do any of you men also speak English?"

No one responded. "Well, what were you braves a doin over here in these parts anyway? How'd you git off the reservation?" he asked, but only their spokesman responded.

"No speaky good English," he said.

"Hayden!" the sheriff called out. "Come up here, will you? You speak this Comanche lingo, don't you?"

"Sure do, Sheriff," Hayden said, riding up alongside.

"Good. Now, Hayden, it's clear that the one who speaks a little English doesn't speak enough to give us a clear explanation of their situation. So ask these renegades what in the hell they're a doing so far off the reservation. Keep talkin till you git the truth out of 'em."

"I'll see what I can do, Sheriff." As a teenager Jim Hayden had spent a couple years on a Comanche reservation with his father, a government Indian agent back in those days, and had taken up with the Indian boys his age and had learned to speak their language fluently. Turning to the Indian spokesman, he surprised him by greeting him in Comanche. The Indians were amazed that a white man could speak their language so well.

Just then another of the braves suddenly called out "Hayden!" and, all smiles, came riding up front.

Seeing him, Hayden exclaimed in astonishment, "Teneefe!" The two men quickly dismounted and shook hands, both of them smiling with the excitement of the moment. On the reservation they had been best friends. "Teneefe," Hayden asked his long-lost pal, "how are you anyway, old buddy?"

"Oh, I'm fine, I guess, but we run into heap big trouble yesterday."

"Trouble? What kind of trouble, my Friend?"

"A big bunch of Mexicans snuck up on us early in the morning and caught us without our guns. After the shootin stopped, about half of our men wuz dead. The rest of us wuz forced to hightail it outa there as fast as we could, all of us without weapons. Fortunately, we managed to ketch our horses; and right now we been on our way to tell the sheriff about the attack. We wuz all innocent and minding our business when them fellers from down across the border just opened fire on us."

"I'm very sorry to hear this, Teneefe," Hayden said. Then turning to the sheriff, he told what he had just learned.

"Ask him, Hayden," the sheriff said, "where this took place."

Questioning his Comanche friend further, Hayden then told the sherrif that the attack had occurred about fifteen or twenty miles up in the mountains due east of Eagle Bluff and that this bunch of Indians had just come from there.

"Hayden," Sheriff Anderson said, "have your friend tell us why all these fellers are so far off the reservation."

After questioning Teneefe, Hayden said, "Sheriff, they're all ticked off at the deplorable conditions on the reservation. The land is worthless for farming, and most of the water they had at first has been diverted to the white man's fields. From what I can find out, these braves started on a hunting expedition and, after discussing the bad conditions on the reservation, said, 'To hell with it. We're gonna leave, and we'll come back when we git good and ready.' Their encounter with the Mexicans was like a bolt outa the blue. Caught 'em all off guard."

"I see," the sheriff said, then added, "tell your Comanche friend that I'd like him to come with us and show us where this sorry incident took place. Tell the rest of the braves to go down to Eagle Bluff and wait for us there. Tell them that we will need them to serve as witnesses."

After Hayden had conveyed the sheriff's orders, the Comanches rode off toward Eagle Bluff, leaving Teneefe, to act as guide for the posse. All the while Hayden and his Indian friend were busy jabbering away in an attempt to catch up on lost years.

After about a three-hour ride, for they were heading up into the mountains, the posse arrived at the scene of the carnage. The sheriff and his men counted eight braves dead. "Hayden," Teneefe explained, unable to conceal his sadness at the loss of his friends, "the shots wuz fired from right over there. They come so fast and furious that we didn't even have time to grab our guns. The rest of us dashed back into the timber while one of our men tried to sneak back to pick up his weapon, but he never made it. He joined the dead. Remember Five Moons?"

"I certainly do," Hayden said. "Is he among the dead?"

"I'm sorry to have to answer yes," Teneefe said, his voice breaking. "That's him lying right over there."

Dismounting and walking over to the prostrate and very still body, Hayden recognized the man. Turning to the sheriff, who had followed him over to take a look, he said sadly, "Sheriff, this fellow, 'Five Moons' we called him, was another of my friends. This is absolutely horrible."

"That it is, Hayden," Sheriff Anderson said. "I'm very sorry for what appears to have been a senseless slaughter." Then addressing the rest of the posse, most of them having moved over to take a look at the dead Comanche, the sheriff said, "Men, we're all witnesses to this carnage. We're gonna have to go back to town and question the rest of them Indians individually to see if they all tell the same story. Then we'll proceed from there. Meantime, Sheriff Lawson and his party will be well up into the mountains by now, and chances are that they'll be able to overtake that big band of Mexican hoodlums. If they're the ones that slaughtered these Comanches, Lawson and his men had better be very careful. They themselves could end up in a hornet's nest. It's beginning to look like we might have to call in an army company to settle this issue. . . ."

Sanchez and party somehow had managed to elude Sheriff Lawson and his men from Camarra. They'd continued more or less due east while the three Mexicans were bearing northeast. Two days later as the three were passing just inside the timber at the edge of a large meadow, a shrill and commanding voice rang out. "You men over there, STAY RIGHT WHERE YOU ARE!"

Spotting Sheriff Bronson and the members of his posse rapidly approaching, all of them from Stevensville, Sanchez said, "Quick, Jose! Hide all the extra rifles over in those bushes!"

No sooner had Jose gotten back on his horse when Bronson and his men came riding up. "What are you fellers doing here anyway?" the sheriff demanded.

Replying calmly and in fluent English, Sanchez said, "We're on our way up into the Four Corners country, where we've been hired to work in a coal mine. That's hard coal up there, you know."

"Is that so?" Bronson said. "And how do we know if you're telling the truth?"

"Well, right in the spur of the moment, Sir, I don't exactly know," Sanchez said, "other than the fact that we have brought our own picks and shovels along. You can take a look in the packbag of that little burro right there."

Dismounting and walking back to Susie to have a look, the sheriff, along with a couple of his deputies, examined the two picks and three shovels, then proceeded to examine the rest of the packs. Seeing the crate containing El Nino, he said, "What in the hell do you have in this pack here?"

Laughing, Sanchez said, "You might not be inclined to believe it, Sir, but we promised our partners at the mine to bring them a big block of blue cheese."

"Blue cheese!" Bronson said disbelieving.

"That's right, Sir," Sanchez added smiling, "blue cheese. But I fear that before we get there it will be more than blue. That, however, is just the way our partners like it. Keeps the flies and mosquitos away! The distance is far greater than either of us had imagined, so I'm sure our partners will have their wish as far as the condition the cheese is in by then."

Studying Sanchez for a monent, Bronson asked, "How is it that you speak English so fluently? You don't even have the typical Mexican accent."

"Well, thank you for the compliment, Sir," Sanchez said smiling. "I worked for a couple years down in Columbus, New Mexico, during which time I devoted considerable effort to learning and perfecting my knowledge of the King's English. My tutor, God rest his soul, was a perfectionist; and he drilled me day after day until I had lost my accent. And, of course, I associated freely with the good people of Columbus, all of whom were astounded at my ability to sound like an educated native American. That, essentially, is how I learned your beautiful English language."

"That's all very interesting," Bronson said, "and it's clear that you're not an ignorant man. In fact, you're so smooth as to arouse my suspicions."

"How so?" Sanchez asked, his facial expression belying his amazement. "Your suspicions of what, Sir?"

"Of you three fellers."

"I'm afraid, Sir, that you have us at a distinct disadvantage. We haven't the foggiest idea what you might be driving at."

"Well," Bronson began, "it's like this. We've had a report of some killings, and they involved Mexicans. So how do we know that you fellers weren't mixed up in this situation?"

"About any killings, Sir, we're totally unaware. However, a couple or three days ago we came within a quarter of a mile of crossing paths with a bunch of Mexicans, roughly a dozen we counted. Aware that the pack instinct often takes over, we deemed it wise to stay out of sight. After all, we've come too far to have any kind of untoward incident limit or, at worst, destroy our stated endeavor. Now whether or not those Mexicans might have been involved in any killings is beyond our power to say. We simply don't know. But we sincerely regret any killing that may have taken place."

"I see," Bronson said. "Now one thing puzzles me. Since you're obviously an educated man, why would you throw in with a bunch of coal miners so far away from your home? And, by the way, where is your home?"

"All three of us, Sir, are from Ascension, a little town just over the border from Columbus."

"I know the place," Bronson said smiling. "I had occasion to visit the town some years ago. At that time there was phenomenal excitement about a gold statue called El Nino, the Christ Child. It was said that people came from both near and far to be healed, supposedly, by merely gazing at that statue. Before leaving Ascension, I decided to go to the Church of the Holy Mother, or whatever it was called, and observe for a while. And would you believe that that very morning a sad specimen of a man, a congenital cripple they said, was carried on a stretcher to the church, and after about thirty minutes---now, mind you, I saw this with my own two eyes---after about thirty minutes or so that same man, his body twisted and contorted as he was carried into the church on a stretcher, came running out of the cathedral half-crying and yelling at the top of his lungs something to the effect that, as near as my humble Spanish permitted me to comprehend, 'PRAISE BE TO GOD! PRAISE BE TO GOD AND TO EL NINO, FOR I WENT INTO THE CHURCH HALF A MAN, BUT LOOK AT ME NOW! YES, JUST LOOK AT ME NOW!' I wanna tell you that a holy hush came over the whole area as if the place was bathed in a kind of heavenly light. Now, I'll say one thing about that experience. If I ever end up a cripple or an invalid of some kind, my first and foremost request will be to be taken directly to that church in Ascension!"

Smiling, Sanchez said, "Sir, we know first-handed that what you have just said is true, for we ourselves have observed similar incidents, as have members of the entire community."

"Some Italian, they said, had come all the way from Italy to sculpt that statue," Bronson observed. "All I can say is that he must have been one helluva sculptor."

"That he was," Sanchez noted. "My two friends and I were privileged to see that man, a fellow by name of Arturo; and, to the amazement of all, he was a singularly humble man. Needless to say, he certainly left a lasting mark on the little town of Ascension. Indeed, he put our little town on the map of the world."

"Well, sir," Bronson said smiling, "we've enjoyed meeting you gentlemen and having this friendly little exchange with you. Either you're totally sincere, or you're one helluva consummate liar!" This last remark elicited some hearty laughter from Bronson and the rest of the posse, so Sanchez quickly glanced at his two partners, and then all three of them joined in the laughter.

"You're a kind man, Sir," Sanchez added. "We, too, must say that this conversation has been most refreshing, for we've had virtually no opportunity to visit with anyone since leaving Ascension. By the way, Sir, might I ask what your name is? I want to be able to remember you by name."

"I'm Sheriff Bronson from Stevensville, which is twenty or so miles west of here."

"Thank you, Sir," Sanchez said. "I will remember our pleasant conversation."

"And you, Sir," Bronson said, "what is your name---just for the record?"

"My name," Sanchez said confidently, "is Jorge Garcia. Practically everyone in Ascension knows me."

"Fine," Bronson said smiling. "Good luck to you fellows, and be sure to keep your noses clean!" This latter idiom left Sanchez guessing, but he smiled and said thank you. "And one other thing," the sheriff added, "tell your partners up at the mine that they'd better have plenty of water on hand before they bite into that cheese, for I can guarantee you that it's gonna bite back! . . ."

After the sheriff and his men had left, Sanchez and party made as if they, too, were headed out toward Four Corners, but they went only a short distance where, concealed behind a stand of pines, they could watch the posse disappear. Then they waited till Jose had gone back with Susie to retrieve the confiscated rifles. Then looking at one another and wiping their brows, they practically sighed with relief. "Another close call," Sanchez observed. "Too close in fact for the least bit of comfort. At least the sheriff, once he had engaged us in conversation, turned out to be a reasonable man." Sanchez took time to brief Julio and Jose on the main points of the conversation, just in case they should be overtaken by the sheriff and his men and questioned separately. But that, fortunately, didn't happen.

How the two other sheriffs solved their cases, if at all, Sanchez and partners never did hear and apparently felt it wise not to ask any questions whatsoever relating to those sorry incidents. They continued to bear northeast for about twenty miles, then again headed in a northwesterly direction. Much of the territory they were forced to traverse was dry, cactus-laden, and generally uninviting. Their dwindling food supplies now forced them to be on the lookout for game such as rabbits, sage hen, grouse, wild turkeys, and of course deer, all of which seemed to be abundant. And, crack shots that these three men were, they didn't want for this kind of grub, but their flour by now was depleted, which meant that they were unable to prepare tortillas.

After a number of days their travels took them across the line into Arizona even though at the time they were quite unaware of having passed into another state. Water not always being plentiful in this part of the country, they were forced from time to time to suck the juice out of pieces of cactus from which they had cut off the skin to avoid being pricked by the sharp, barbed needles. They likewise had to prepare strips of cactus for their animals to chew to extract the life-saving juices. At first their horses, mules, and burros didn't want to oblige, but after another day or two without water they no longer needed coaxing.

Steadily bearing off to the west, they came upon a river, whose name they didn't know. But since it flowed north, the direction they were headed, they wisely chose to follow it so they no longer had to suck pieces of cactus to keep from drying up and blowing away. Finding the river to be well endowed with native trout, they were pleased to supplement their diet with fish, which they roasted over hot coals. Sometimes they dug a hole and filled it part-way with hot coals, then placed their trout on the coals and covered them with other coals. The upper layer of coals they then covered with a layer of dirt and sometimes left until morning. Being Mexicans, they were not used to eating fish for breakfast, but after the first morning when they uncovered their trout, the aroma was so tantalizing that they made this unusual cuisine a regular practice wherever they found fish. Some of the "four-footed" grub they prepared in like manner. Indeed, one day Julio shot a large porcupine, which they roasted deep-pit barbecue style until morning. And even though they had not bothered to gut it beforehand, they found it to be a delicacy, for all of the creature's needles had been burned off, leaving the meat juicy and tender. Naturally, they stayed clear of the animal's cooked entrails, which didn't seem to have affected the rest of the edible meat. "When man is forced to forage in the wilderness," Julio said laughing, "he must make do with whatever nature provides."

Rattlesnakes, too, were plentiful; and from time to time the men roasted one, naturally after cutting off its dangerous head (which contains the sack of virulent poison) and skinning the fear-inspiring reptile. "Tastes remarkably like chicken," Jose observed. But they preferred chicken---prairie chicken---and grouse and sage hen to rattlesnake. One morning while attempting to catch some fish in the river, they startled a duck, which flew off quacking unhappily, for she had just added another egg to her nest, making six eggs in all. Rationalizing that the mother duck would have no trouble laying six more eggs, they took their booty and feasted on eggs for breakfast.

One moonlit night when their animals suddenly began to snort and make peculiar noises, all three men jumped out of bed and, each with a rifle in hand, went running barefoot to see what was causing the problem. Just as they got to where their animals were staked out for the night, gentle little Susie screamed with terror as a very large cougar ripped open her jugular vein and wrestled her to the ground. Thanks to the bright moonlight, three shots rang out simultaneously, one of the slugs passing through the predator's skull from behind. Jose, who was very partial to their little burro Susie, rushed up to where the cougar was breathing its last and, half crying and cussing, fired several more shots into the predator's head. It was an emotional moment for all three men, for their little Susie had been especially faithful and docile throughout the entire trip.

Turning to look at the burro, they saw the sad little creature lying drenched in her still-warm blood. Glancing back at the cougar, Jose said, "Let's leave the dastardly beast lying there till morning. Then I'll skin it out."

After getting their other animals calmed down, the three men went back and wrapped themselves in their blankets, for although the days were very warm, the nights at such high altitudes are always chilly. Jose, however, terribly distraught at losing Susie, couldn't sleep. So taking his blanket and positioning himself on a large flat rock near her remains, he sat rifle in hand the rest of the night protecting her body from other predators. Long about the time when the first rays of light came venturing into this part of the sky, Jose, upwind from a coyote,

86

sat silently watching the creature make its way up to sniff around Susie's carcass. Taking careful aim, he fired a slug into the coyote's brain, causing the wily creature to spring about five feet into the air. Crashing back to earth in a lifeless heap, this second predator---another of nature's children---quite literally had bitten the dust. Jose stepped cautiously toward the coyote to inspect it and noticed that its eyes already had the unmistakable glaze of death in them, and blood was running out of the animal's mouth and nostrils. Cursing the coyote for its audacity to approach Susie to feed off her carcass, Jose leaned his rifle against a tree, then picked the body up by the hindlegs and hurled it with all of his strength out into the sagebrush. "There, you wretched critter!" he said in anger. "Perhaps you and the cougar, mortal enemies though you've been here in mortality, might want to get together and compare notes to see which one of you was the more stupid!" Thus, in his way Jose assisted nature in providing a meal or two for other four-footed predators, be they wolves or coyotes, both of these breeds, coyotes in particular, being well represented in those parts. Indeed, from time to time when a coyote tended to be a bit brazen, he was duly treated with some hot lead between the eyes. Truly the wilderness can be a very harsh place not only for animals but also for men who venture out into wild and untamed country.

When morning came, the men were up and about tending to their animals, leading them down to the river to get a drink of the pure mountain water. This done, Sanchez and Julio, shovel in hand, proceeded to dig a grave for Susie while Jose busied himself in skinning the cougar, whose carcass he then rolled out into the sagebrush to be devoured by other predators. Nature is remarkably efficient in seeing that nothing goes to waste.

Holding the cougar pelt up triumphantly, Jose said, "We will cover Susie with this pelt, the pelt of her murderer, to serve henceforth as her protector." Then after a moment or two of reflection, he added, "What supreme irony we see here with the creature who so viciously took her life now serving---quite obviously against his wishes---as her protector in death." And so the three men tenderly lowered Susie's body into the freshly dug grave, after which Jose meticulously, if not somewhat mysteriously, placed the cougar pelt over Susie's mortal remains. His voice breaking, he said, "She was an exceptionally faithful and gentle little animal. I'll never forget her." And then they covered the grave and rolled some large stones over the spot to serve as a deterrent to any predators that might try to uncover her carcass. . . .

NAVAJOS

Their long journey continued, but Susie's absence they keenly felt. Jose, as if lost in thought, was silent most of that first day after the tragedy.

Having traveled in a northwesterly direction now for several days, they soon would be crossing over into Utah just west of Four Corners, the only spot in the continental United States where one can stand in four states at the same time. This they knew was Navajo country although they hadn't had any person-to-person contact with any of these Indians. True, at different times the past few days they had seen small bands of them from a distance, but the Navajos apparently hadn't seen them. Or if they had seen them, they didn't let it be known, a tactic not uncommon among America's native peoples.

One morning just after shooting a deer and skinning it out, they were busily engaged in cutting thin strips of the buckmeat and spreading them out on a tarp they had laid on the ground. Turning these strips of meat over every hour or so would mean that, given the intensity of the sun's rays in that part of the country that time of the year, they'd have a good supply of jerky by evening. This they would bag up and treat themselves to the delicious dried meat whenever they felt the urge. But after covering the tarp with strips of meat, they still had much of the venison left, more than they could eat before it spoiled on them; and they were wondering whether to try to take it with them or simply to leave it there for any hungry predators that happened along.

Their problem appeared to be solved, however, when they suddenly looked up to discover some visitors---eight or ten Navajos on horseback. One of their own horses had whinnied moments earlier, but the three Mexicans had gone right on placing the strips of venison on the tarp to dry. Sanchez, quickly raising his hand in a friendly salute, said in English, "Good morning, gentlemen! You're just in time to enjoy the rest of this venison, which is more than we can handle. We were contemplating leaving it here for any natural predators that might come along. As you can see, we're in the process of making us some jerky to nibble on as we continue our journey over into the Buckskin Mountains. All of our flour has been gone for more than two weeks, and we've been subsisting on meat, fish, fowl, and occasional duck eggs."

After what seemed like much too long a pause, the spokesman for the Navajos, a young man in perhaps his late twenties, finally responded. "You are Mexicans, are you not?"

"Yes, we're Mexicans from the little town of Ascension just over the New Mexico/Mexican border in the state of Chihuahua. We are on our way to the Buckskin Mountains to join some friends in a coal-mining venture. For that reason we are passing through this part of the country. "

"If you're a Mexican," the Navajo spokesman said to Sanchez, "how is it that you speak English so well. You don't sound like a Mexican to me."

"The compliment I appreciate, my Friend, but I am a Mexican; and my two friends likewise are Mexicans. However, they don't speak any English other than just a few isolated words. As to why I speak English fluently, I spent two years working in Columbus, New Mexico, for a wealthy family who were kind enough to hire a very competent tutor to teach me to speak English without an accent. This, simply stated, is why I have no Mexican accent. I should like to return the compliment to you, for you speak surprisingly good English. Have you attended school among the white people?"

"As a matter of fact I have, and it is my intention to graduate from college; I've already had two years of college."

"I'm not surprised to hear this," Sanchez said smiling. "My compliments to you."

"And you say you're heading over into Utah's Buckskin Mountains?"

"Correct. It's been a long journey. Perhaps you could tell us the best way to get across the Colorado."

"A simple matter," the Navajo said. "Just swim your horses across and hold to their tails; horses being excellent swimmers, they'll pull you right across. We Navajos do this all the time whenever we go up to Escalante and some of those small towns to do some horse trading or to sell saddles, bridles, hackamores, blankets, rugs, and jewelry."

"Yes, we've heard that the Navajos are very skilled at crossing the river in this manner, but we have a slight problem. You see, we have a large block of blue cheese packed in a crate in one of our packbags, and the cheese would be ruined if it got wet, which it invariably would if we swam our horses across the river the way you gentlemen do. Consequently, we must find someone along the river with a boat so we can get the cheese across without damaging it. We've transported it all the way from Ascension, and to spoil it now that we're this close to our goal would be heart-breaking, at least for our friends who are waiting expectantly for this their favorite cheese!"

"I see your problem," the Navajo said. "Chances are that you might well find someone with a boat along that section of the river just south of where the San Juan empties into the Colorado. And now you say you'd like to share the venison with us?"

"That's right. It's more than we can eat, and it would be a shame to waste it simply because we can't eat all of it before it goes bad. We'd be honored to give it to you gentlemen if you'll accept it." Two of the Indians rode over to where the rest of the deer carcass was suspended from a large juniper and, after cutting the carcass in two, proceeded to load it onto their horses. Sanchez, noting the deer hide, said, "And you're welcome to take this hide also. Smiling, another of the braves hopped off his horse and rolled up the hide and secured it behind his saddle.

"Thank you," the Navajo spokesman said. "And, by the way, how long do you propose to remain right here before moving on?"

"Probably most, if not all, of the day. At least until this jerky dries enough that we can bag it up and be on our way."

"Don't leave until we return." Thus speaking, the Navajo motioned for his friends to follow; and, waving as they rode off, they quickly disappeared into that rugged country, where the junipers are so thick in places that a man has to keep his sights on a distant mountain peak or an otherwise visible landmark to maintain his course.

Not knowing what to expect, Sanchez and partners finished placing the last venison strips on the tarp to dry and then cleaned their knives first by jabbing them into the ground three or four times and then wiping them off on the branch of a juniper, after which they replaced them in their scabbards. Positioning themselves so that they would have immediate access to their rifles in case of trouble, they waited semi-impatiently for thirty or so minutes when suddenly the Navajos reappeared, this time with a large bag of something resting in front of one Indian's saddle horn. Smiling, the spokesman got off his horse and, taking the sack into his arms, presented it to Sanchez. "You said you'd been out of flour for a couple weeks or so. Here's a hundred pounds of flour. Enjoy it!"

Overwhelmed at this generous offer, Sanchez extended his hand to the spokesman and said, "Many, many thanks to you and your friends. Please convey to them our heart-felt appreciation. This flour we indeed will enjoy."

"We hope so," the Navajo said smiling. "After all, it's home grown and stone ground and it makes some of the most wonderful biscuits you've ever tasted. Nothing's finer than a strip of fried or roasted buckmeat or mutton inside one of those hot biscuits."

"You have our mouths watering already, my Friend," Sanchez said. "Thank you so very much."

"No thanks necessary," the Navajo said. "One good deed begets another. Or as the English say, 'A fair exchange is no robbery!'

"I need no further convincing that you're a college man!" Sanchez said laughing. And the rest of the Navajos, noting the spirit of levity, also joined in the laughter.

"We must be on our way now," the Navajo said. "We wish you gentlemen godspeed, and do be careful not to get your cheese wet! . . ."

"Incredible. Utterly incredible," Sanchez said to Julio and Jose, both of whom readily agreed. "First we encounter four white hunters, smart alecks all of them, ol' Big Mouth in particular. And those jerkos would have killed us if they could have had their way. Then we're attacked by a larger band of gringos who start shooting without asking any questions. What we didn't know and they didn't know either is that just a short distance west of us some twelve or fifteen Comanches were camped out; and when a stray bullet hit and killed one of their braves, the Comanches started shooting and killed most of the gringos. Then discovering us, the Comanches began playing a little cat and mouse game, which ended with us being relieved of our horses and goods, El Nino in particular. Then through some luck, good fortune, or perhaps some help from up above, we managed to retrieve our animals and goods **and** El Nino, after which, for better or for worse, we dispatched a number of the braves into the Happy Hunting Grounds, where guns and arrows and knives and treachery no longer have any effect. Finally, we meet up with these Navajos, who have met us with pure Christian kindness. What else is likely to happen to us before we reach our ultimate goal?"

After this encounter with the friendly Navajos, they felt self-assured that fortune was smiling down upon them; and so they spent the day leisurely, every hour or so turning over the strips of drying jerky and letting their animals enjoy a much-needed rest. By late afternoon the powerful desert sun had worked its wonders with the meat, and the three men were just getting ready to bag the jerky when a shot rang out, the powerful slug kicking up a little cloud of dust just two or three feet away from them and then ricocheting against several large boulders nearby. Startled, they had no time to grab a rifle, but all of them had a pistol concealed under their clothing.

Three young Navajos ranging in age from sixteen to eighteen, all three astride their ponies, sat with rifles trained on the unsuspecting men. "All right, Mexicanos," their apparent leader called out imperiously, "down on your bellies right now if you know what's good for you. NOW! I said. And don't make me have to ask you a second time, for there will be no second time for you!"

Calling the punk's bluff, Sanchez smiled and said, "What, pray tell, is the meaning of this? Just this morning we had a very friendly visit with several members of your tribe, the leader quite obviously a college man. We gave them the remaining half of a deer we had just killed this morning, and about forty-five minutes later they returned with a 100-pound sack of flour for us and wished us well."

"Look," the spokesman said, brandishing his weapon threateningly, "I don't give a hoot for all that goody goody crap. Now git down on your bellies right now, all three of you, or we will be forced to give you some unwanted assistance."

Still calling the young Navajo's bluff, Sanchez said calmly, "I can tell by the words you're using that you've been to a white man's school, haven't you?"

"And if I have, Mexicano, what the hell's that to you?"

"Well, I can't help wondering," Sanchez observed, "if the dangerous course you three young men are pursuing right now is something you were taught in school. Surely it wasn't. And what would your elders think if they knew that you three are up to this skullduggery? Would they praise you for it?"

"What our elders might think or do is no concern of ours and certainly no concern of yours either."

"You seriously don't think so?" Sanchez asked. "Then what would you three fellows do if some of your elders, having gotten wind of your---shall we say ---irregular activity of the moment should come riding up behind you, weapons drawn?"

"Look, Mexicano," the young Navajo said, "you're trying to distract us, but we will be neither distracted nor confused by anything you say. Now lay down right now and don't let me have to tell you again. You've tried my patience already."

"To distract you is precisely what we're trying to do," Sanchez said, still unintimidated. "Through this friendly little dialogue we're hoping that the light of reason might penetrate your brains sufficiently to let you see that what you're attempting to do is extremely unwise. What, for instance, do you hope to gain by having us lie down so you can tie our hands and feet? Are you hoping to steal our animals and our humble goods and then leave us to rot out here in the desert sun? Have you forgotten that some of your elders spent several minutes with us and had a chance to take a close look at our animals? So if all of a sudden you three young men should show up back at the reservation with these animals, don't you think your elders would recognize them immediately? You, for sure, would be severely disciplined for your actions, would you not? Besides, you don't know us from Adam. And if you did, I can assure you that to harm or even kill us and to steal our animals and our goods would be the farthest things from your minds. Now, tell me, my young Friends, if this doesn't make very good sense to you."

"All right, Mexicano," the young hothead said, "yes, what you say makes sense. You're clever with words, but you're not clever enough to keep us from doing what we intend to do. Now git down on your bellies right now and stop all that blabbering 'cause it aint gonna do you no good no how."

"Tell you what, young fella," Sanchez said, "before you do anything drastic or just plain stupid, and to save you the trouble of tying all three of us up, why don't you appoint one of your friends there to guard us while two of you go to inspect our animals? Then you can come and take a look at our gear. We clearly don't have much---just a couple or three picks and shovels that we'll need when we get over into the Buckskin Mountains to join some friends at a newly opened coal mine. And, yes, we have a large block of blue cheese in one of the packs. Believe it or not, we've transported this all the way from northern Mexico as a special treat for our waiting friends. We request most humbly that you don't disturb the packaging around the cheese."

"Mexicano, how in the hell do you speak such good English anyway? You could talk the friggin bark right off these junipers."

"My young Friend," Sanchez replied, "I'm merely trying to get you and your partners to see the error of your ways. What kind of world would you envision if everyone in it should start behaving like you? Think about it. In all seriousness, would you be happy and content in such a world? Would you be content in a world where everyone was out to get you? Would you be content if you couldn't lay anything down and go off and leave it for any length of time for fear that it wouldn't be there when you returned? Would you like that kind of world? Or would it not be a wonderful and self-assuring place if you could trust your neighbor? And if your neighbor in turn could trust you? Would it not be marvelous if your neighbor looked out for your best interests instead of trying to take advantage of you? And would not you yourself beam with satisfaction to realize that instead of taking advantage of your neighbor you were looking out for his best interests, so long of course as they were legitimate interests?"

"Yes, of course, Mexicano. I'm not stupid. But by the same token, you're not going to talk us out of what we came here to do."

"And what exactly is it that you plan to do?"

Laughing, the young Navajo said, "We might just as well say it because there's nothing whatsoever that you can say, clever talker though you may be, to stop us. We're going to take your animals, all your goods, and then tie the three of you up to one of these junipers and leave you to be devoured by the wolves and coyotes!"

"Well, now," Sanchez said smiling, "what big brave fellows you three are, all three of you sitting there with loaded rifles trained on us three innocent men, men who have never harmed a hair of your head and, frankly, don't intend to. My, my, I'll bet your mothers and fathers would be proud of you right at this moment if they were hidden behind one of these rocks watching you and taking in this conversation. Do you think they might be inclined to disown you? Maybe even to send you out into the dry and barren desert and tell you not to come back until you had straightened up and decided to be gentlemen worthy of your good parents and the other honorable members of your tribe?"

"To hell with your unending supply of words! Now LAY DOWN RIGHT NOW! ALL THREE OF YOU BEFORE YOU FORCE US TO DO SOMETHING DRASTIC!"

"Tell you what," Sanchez said half chuckling. "All three of you fellows appear to be in good physical shape. You're good athletes. I can see it written all over you, and it's clear that you're physically very strong. Now let's see if we can cut a little deal here. With one of your partners acting as guard to see that my two friends don't interfere, why don't you and your other partner put your rifles back in their scabbards and take me on in

96

a wrestling match? Both of you at the same time. Surely you two big huskies ought to be able to pin me to the ground in a mere matter of seconds, right? And not only that, but just think how popular the two of you will be back at the reservation to be able to tell your friends how you tied a smart-mouthed Mexican up in knots and left him to wither in the wind and eventually to blow away! How 'bout it, gentlemen? Are you game? Two on one! The two of you fighting me. Not bad odds, wouldn't you say?"

The two men looking at one another, the spokesman grinned and said, "Sure. Why not? That'll be one sure way to silence you. Why, hell, we haven't been able to do a damned thing because you just keep talking. Sure, we'll take you on, Mexicano. Someone needs to teach you a lesson in listening instead of talking so damned much!" And having said this, the spokesman and one of his partners replaced their rifles in their scabbards and hopped off their horses.

Meantime, Sanchez quickly did some bending and stretching exercises and, smiling, motioned for the two young Navajos to have at him. Somewhat cautiously they approached, then suddenly lunged for him. But Sanchez, like greased lightning, grabbed both men by the hair and, turning their faces toward one another, rammed their foreheads together and at the precise moment of impact came up with his right knee in time to connect with each one's chin, lifting both men into the air and landing each one on the back of his head. Then before either man could get his bearings, Sanchez again seized them by the hair and, jerking them onto their feet, rammed their heads together again, the severe thud echoing on the surrounding boulders as the two braves again bit the dust. Then, with both young men incapacitated, Sanchez grabbed the spokesman by his two braids and, whirling him a couple times, sent him flying out into the sagebrush, where he landed face first, his nose plowing a neat little furrow out through the soft dirt. Then quickly grabbing the other decommissioned brave, he repeated the same action, sending him flying out into the sagebrush, where he landed quite miraculously alongside his partner.

Meantime, the third brave, the guard (!), had turned his horse around and hightailed it out of there, but he didn't get too far before being overtaken by the same group of Navajo elders who had delivered the 100-pound sack of flour earlier. Moments later they returned to where Sanchez, Julio, and Jose were waiting.

"Where'd those two other fellers go?" the original spokesman asked, his voice edged with anger.

Pointing, Sanchez said, "They're both lying right out there. You see, they challenged me to a little wrestling match, fully confident that both of them together could throw me to the ground in a mere matter of seconds, after which they intended to rob us of everything and then leave me and my two partners tied up out here to die. I tried my best to talk them out of this madness, but all three of them had loaded rifles trained on us. Unable to dissuade them, I finally offered to take two of 'em on at the same time while the third one stood guard to see that neither of my partners interfered."

At about this time, first the one and then the other of the braves began to stir out in the sagebrush. The spokesman and the rest of his party got off their horses to have a firsthand look. Suddenly one of the Navajos started pointing and laughing uncontrollably. "That's my son!" he said. "That's my Thomas! Look at him! Hey, Thomas, what in the hell are you doing a layin out there anyway? Huh, Thomas!" he said, still unable to control his laughter. Then turning to his partners, he said, "This, without a doubt, is the greatest thing that's ever happened to my hot-tempered and bull-headed son! Hey, Thomas," he said tauntingly, "has Mister Know it All learned anything today?"

Thomas, sitting up by now and rubbing his eyes and shaking the dirt out of his hair, said nothing. His humiliation was complete. The lesson of literal hard knocks that he'd learned today he'd never ever forget.

"And you, Owl Face," his uncle asked, "have you likewise learned a lasting lesson just now? What big brave fellers the two of you are! The two of you against this man over here!"

Then another of the Navajo elders spoke. "And there sits my big brave Johnny, much too smart to listen to either me or his mother. What in the sam hell did you plan to do, boy! Did you actually plan to shoot these three innocent men and then to rob them of their animals and goods? You three young smart asses have brought shame upon all of us. We've tried to teach you correct principles so that you would govern yourselves as men, but you've behaved today like cowardly and worthless sissies, neither of you worthy to be called a Navajo! Have you forgotten what the word Navajo means, huh? For your information, punks, it means THE PEOPLE! And we are a proud and honorable PEOPLE, and none of us in any way, shape, or form appreciates how you three have disgraced us this day. Now we want all three of you to come and stand before these honorable gentlemen and tell them how very sorry you are for your abominable actions. That's right! Git right over here. Off your horse, Johnny! Now, we want to hear each one of you individually apologize to these three gentlemen, who of their own free will and choice were kind enough to share that fresh venison with us this morning. For your information, we consider these three men our friends. They're passing peacefully through our territory; and we, consequently, owe them every courtesy! . . ."

Speaking of this incident several days later, Sanchez said, "I still have to pinch myself and ask if all of that really happened or if I was dreaming. The courtesy and kindness of those Navajo men is still overwhelming to me. I can speak of them only in superlatives. Indeed, I'd stand by men like them through thick and thin. That encounter will always be a high point in my life, for I quite frankly didn't know that such men could possibly inhabit these waste places."

"It was all like a revelation to me, too," Jose commented. "I'm grateful, Sanchez, that you had presence of mind to challenge those showoffs to a wrestling match. I was beginning to feel somewhat desperate. Naturally, I didn't want to have to start shooting, especially at such young and inexperienced men as those three. But if push had come to shove, I'd have opened fire. As it was, the push had already started, and the shove was just waiting to happen."

"My thoughts, too," Julio said. "I wish there was something in our power we could do to show our appreciation for such kindness. Perhaps God will let the beneficent influence of El Nino radiate over this entire area, healing those who are sick or starving or discouraged or disparing. Surely something of this nature will occur because of the kindness displayed toward us by those Najavo men. And, who knows? Perhaps this incident might have been foreseen as a means of getting those three young men back onto the right track. They'll remember the shaking up that you gave them, Sanchez! In all honesty I must congratulate you on that spectacular performance. Looking back, I believe the inconvenience of that hour was well worth it just to see you swing into action!"

"Kind words, my Friend," Sanchez said grinning. "Once a man has had martial arts principles drilled into him, he rarely ever forgets them. They've saved my hide a number of times, and I trust that they'll continue to do so. I try not to pick a fight, but at the same time I don't run from one either!"

By now this party of three from Ascension had entered the spectacular Monument Valley of Utah, where great sandrock sentinels dotted the landscape and seemed to greet the occasional visitor by day and to stand guard over that sacred territory by night. And hot as the days had become, night was always a pleasurable time both for men and beasts, whether the latter were domesticated or wild. Whenever the moon was full, coyotes and their cousins the wolves could be heard barking and howling their messages, whether to one another or to the resplendent moon. The three Mexicans marveled at such stark beauty, attributing the same to the Master Sculptor, who never forgot even the most minute detail. They, fortunately, had filled all of their water bags with river water; and now, traveling through this wonderland of seemingly endless geologic shapes and forms, they had to be sparing with this precious, life-sustaining substance.

Each day the men carried a pocketful of venison jerky, each piece of which they ate very slowly, savoring the tantalizing juice that stilled their hunger pangs. And when they were not eating jerky, each one held a small pebble in the side of his cheek to keep saliva flowing, this tending to slake their thirst. Water at a premium in these parts, they often sliced off the treacherous needles from cacti so their animals could chew and suck the precious juice from the pulp. Each evening after the men had found a bit of forage for their animals, they built a small fire and made their humble tortillas from the flour given them by the Navajos. As yet they still had a bit of coffee left, enough for each of them to have at least one cup with their morning meal and another with their evening meal.

Nights, usually cloudless, were filled with visual splendor out in the midst of the desert, where millions of stars comprising the Milky Way maintained their commanding presence. Virtually every portion of the heavens was studded with great celestial orbs, for the atmosphere in that region and for hundreds of miles around was unburdened with the smoke and debris from industry. Gazing nightly at this vast panorama of twinkling lights, the men often wondered what might be out there in the infinitude of celestial space. "Do you believe," Julio asked one evening just after each of them had wrapped himself in his blanket and stretched out on the ground for a peaceful night's rest, "that other worlds like ours might be out there?"

"Why not?" Jose volunteered. "Perhaps at this very moment someone on a distant planet is asking this same question while scanning the sky and wondering just where another world might be."

"And if it is true that other worlds are out there," Sanchez asked, "do you think that the people inhabiting them might worship the same God that we do?"

"What exactly do you mean, Sanchez?" Julio queried.

"Did not the great Apostle Paul," Sanchez asked, "tell the Corinthians something to the effect that 'there are gods many and lords many, whether in heaven or on earth, but unto us there is only one God, the Father, of whom are all things, and we in him; and one Lord Jesus Christ, by whom are all things, and we by him'?"

"I seem to remember having heard that passage before," Julio commented. "Are you suggesting by it that gods other than our God the Father might be in control in distant worlds?"

"Actually," Sanchez began reflectively, "I'm not sure what I'm suggesting. But I have to admit that this particular passage

101

has always intrigued me. Too bad we don't have Paul here to explain it to us!"

"Having an actual living apostle in our midst for a while," Jose added, "would answer a whole host of questions, wouldn't it? Why is it that nowadays we don't have such a man on the earth who could speak with authority and say, 'Thus saith the Lord'? As it is---and I don't want to sound like a heretic---but there apparently is no such person on the earth right now. Two thousand years ago there were living apostles and prophets, but I don't know of any today. His Holiness the Pope over in Rome says that actual, full-fledged revelation from God to man ceased some two thousand years ago. Today the Pope merely interprets bible passages."

"That's right, Jose," Julio said; "and who is competent enough to know if what he says is actual gospel truth? Since the pronouncement was made to the world in about 1870 that the Pope is fallible, how can we be entirely sure he's telling the truth when he makes a so-called 'infallible' statement?"

Chuckling, Sanchez said, "I can't believe you guys. You've never spoken like this before! Aren't we simply to believe what the Pope says? Too bad Padre de Escalante isn't here with us this evening. He undoubtedly would have a logical answer for us. I have yet to see the time that anyone could stump him. Certainly good ol' Pancho Villa didn't get too far with him! And he tried three times. He might even have tried again in our absence, thinking that perhaps through some miraculous means El Nino again would be resting in the usual place in the cathedral."

"This raises a question that has crossed my mind a number of times as of late," Jose said. "Let's assume (and may God make it so) that we are successful in hiding El Nino in one of those big caves on---did you not say--- 'Grand Bench,' Sanchez?"

"Yes, Jose. That's the sacred place."

"Okay, then," Jose continued, "let's say that we're successful in hiding El Nino in one of those caves. How long do you think it will have to remain there before we or someone else will return to transport it back to the Cathedral of the Blessed Virgin in Ascension?"

"That is a moot question indeed," Sanchez said reflectively. "Just off the top of my head I'd say that political stability must be evident in northern Mexico. So long as Villa or others of his ilk are raising cane in those parts, it would seem to be highly unlikely for El Nino to be brought back. However, down deep I feel that this wondrous statue must be brought back, for there seems to be an endless of supply of sick people who will be seeking the blessings of health and happiness through the good graces of El Nino."

"And exactly how," Julio asked, "will we know which of those caves on Grand Bench will be the right one in which to hide El Nino?"

"Again in the spur of the moment I don't rightly know," Sanchez confessed. "But this much I **do** know---when we enter that particular cave, a manifestation of some kind will be given to let us know that we've found the right spot. Moreover, it will be put into our minds how to conceal the statue and to camouflage its location, for rumor with her thousand tongues will make it known somehow that a precious object is alleged to have been hidden in one of those caves on Grand Bench, which is on the southeast side of the Kaiparowits Plateau. . . ."

Sleep having fled from their eyes, and the night, peaceful and serene with its myriad stars twinkling merrily as if that was all they had to do, plus the fact that they might be harboring myriad worlds out there somewhere, Jose said, "I recall how Moses on two different occasions went up onto Mt. Sinai for forty days and nights to sojourn in the very presence of God. Moreover, John the Baptist prepared for his important ministry by going out into the wilderness for some forty days and nights. And, finally the Savior Himself went into the wilderness for a like period of time to meditate and to prepare Himself spiritually for His unique mission of atoning for the sins of the entire world, something that only He of all the Father's spirit children was capable of doing."

"Sounds almost as if there might be something magical about the figure forty, doesn't it?" Julio said somewhat tongue in cheek.

"The latter part of your comment, Jose, intrigues me," Sanchez noted reflectively. "How exactly did you come up with the thought that Christ was the only One of all the Father's spirit children capable of bringing about the atonement? Does not this concept throw a wrench into the wheel of the Nicene Creed, so called because of the conclusions reached at this decisive meeting of some 318 bishops of the church way back in A.D. 325?"

"For a number of years," Jose confessed, "I've studied the results of this all-important conclave but have not had the nerve to broach the subject with anyone. Out here in this wilderness with you two, whom I count among my very best friends, I don't feel uneasy about mentioning these things although I know, as both of you do likewise, that as Catholics we are admonished simply to accept such teachings on faith rather than to delve into them in an attempt to come up with a logical answer."

"Go on, Jose," Sanchez said. "Never before have I heard you speak in such depth about these things."

Chuckling, Jose said, "My friends, I'm just getting started! Back in A.D. 325 when Constantine, at the time not a Christian, summoned all of the bishops of the church as it had evolved since the time of Christ and the living apostles, some 400 or so bishops if I recall correctly, to hasten to Nicaea in Asia Minor (present-day Turkey), it took months for some of them to make arrangements to get there, the final number turning out to be 318. While the troops were waiting for their compradres of the cloth to arrive, they had to have some entertainment; and two of the bishops, Athanasius and Arius, were eager to display their erudition, specifically their forensic abilities. Hardly before anyone knew it, the subject of debate had gravitated to the composition of the Godhead. Did the same consist of Three separate Personalities or just One? Arius insisted that there were Three: God the Father, God the Son, and God the Holy Spirit, all of them Spirit Entities separate and distinct from one another. Athanasius, on the other hand, insisted that by some incomprehensible means these Three were actually One while at the same time Three, a kind of spiritual blob that finds not one iota of confirmation in the Good Book."

"I see where you're headed," Sanchez observed. "Christ dwelled in the flesh here on earth and, after being crucified and lying in the sepulchre from Friday afternoon until some time before sunrise the following Sunday morning, He arose from the dead, He being the first fruits of them that slept. The first mortal to behold Him in His resurrected state was Mary Magdalene, who, apon recognizing Him that morning, moved toward Him naturally and impulsively as if to embrace Him, but He forbade her, saying, 'Touch me not, for I have not yet ascended unto my Father in heaven. But go and tell my brethren that I live.' This she in greatest excitement did, and throughout the day Jesus appeared intermittently to individuals and small groups. That same evening He culminated His day's activities by appearing to ten of the apostles and apparently some wives and children in the Upper Room in Jerusalem. Naturally they were shocked because the doors and windows were bolted shut, Jerusalem being an unhealthy place for Christians to be during that tempestuous period. To calm their troubled souls, Christ, His hands outstretched to them, said, 'Why are ye affrighted, and why do these thoughts arise in your minds? **Feel me and see, for a spirit hath not flesh and bones as ye see me have?'** And after this little group had gotten over their fright, realizing that He who stood before them was the very Christ, they came forward one by one and gazed into His brilliant eyes while feeling the wounds in His hands and feet and having the Holy Spirit bear solemn and irrefutable witness to them that He was Jesus, the resurrected Savior."

"Precisely!" Jose affirmed. "And during the next forty days ---there's that figure forty again!---He appeared from time to time to individuals and groups, one group in fact said to number at least 500 souls. I might add that in a court of law this would be some mighty hefty evidence in support of His resurrected state. Not only this, but the Good Book says that on the Sunday when Christ was resurrected the graves of many of the saints that slept, ostensibly from the days of Adam and Eve up unto the meridian of time, were opened and the denizens of those graves likewise came forth in the resurrection, their immortal spirits reunited inseparably with the elements comprising their phyusical bodies, and they appeared to many in and around Jerusalem during the next forty days and nights. Then just prior to His ascension into heaven, the resurrected Savior, after walking incognito for some distance from Jerusalem toward Emmaus with two of His disciples, was finally taken up from them. Transfixed, they watched Him disappear into the heavens; and while they were in this reverential attitude, an angel clothed in radiant white said unto them, 'Ye men of Galilee, why stand ye gazing steadfastly into heaven? Know ye not that this same Jesus who has just been taken up from you into heaven will come in like manner in the latter days?' . . . or words to this effect."

"Intensely interesting," Julio commented. "I think I can anticipate where this discussion is leading. You're going to say, are you not, that since Christ ascended bodily into heaven and will descend bodily out of heaven in the latter days, that logically He should be bodily in heaven at this very moment? Am I right in this assessment?"

"Right on the money, Julio," Jose stated excitedly. "And this is where part of the rub comes with the decisions agreed upon in the Council of Nicaea, for the resultant Nicene Creed states emphatically that Father, Son, and Holy Spirit are not Three but One, and not One but Three, having no bodily parts and passions while being large enough to fill the immensity of space and at the same time small enough to dwell in one's heart."

"This raises a whole raft of intriguing questions, doesn't it?" Sanchez commented. "So since the resurrected Savior said, 'Feel me and see, for a spirit hath not flesh and bones as ye see me have,' how could the good bishops back in A.D. 325 have concluded that Father, Son, and Holy Spirit are One in Three and at the same time Three in One? And in the Garden of Gethsemane the night before His crucifixion, how could Jesus have prayed to God the Father if He (Christ) and the Father and the Holy Spirit were actually One and the same Person? This, it seems to me, is tantamount to reducing the theology of the Godhead to a kind of incomprehensible Double Dutch!"

"Furthermore," Julio said, enjoying this most irregular theological discussion, "when the resurrected Savior returns to earth in the latter days to usher in His great Millennial Reign, and people everywhere see Him as He is---a resurrected, glorified Personage, a resurrected MAN if you please, how will the theorists square this incontrovertible fact with the tenets of the Nicene Creed?"

"Well," Sanchez began philosophically, "if we're to apply a nickel's worth of logic to what has just been said---and, I might add, quite eloquently said---we'd have to consign the Nicene Creed to the spiritual dung heap, would we not?!"

After a hearty laugh, the three Mexicans concluded that they had played the role of "heretic" long enough for one night. Then Jose, speaking as if with an afterthought, said, "Then we have our precious statue of El Nino, the Christ Child, whose image was conceptualized by the great Luigi Arturo of Florence, Italy. Doubtlessly, or so it would seem to me, the face of this statue must be similar to that of the Infant Jesus, who grew into manhood, conducted His ministry for some three years, during which time He personally selected and ordained His twelve apostles, was crucified and placed in the tomb where, after a period of some forty or so hours, He arose bodily from the tomb to say, 'Feel me and see, for a spirit hath not flesh and bones as ye see me have.' For the life of me I just can't fathom how the Savior, after going out of His way, as it were, to clarify these indispensable realities, would turn right around again and dissipate into nothingness."

"Indeed, Jose," Sanchez said. "This most unusual of discussions has made a big impression on all of us. Somehow it bolsters my confidence that, one way or another, we will be successful in finding the sacred cave and depositing our precious cargo in it for an unspecified time. Now, what say we all get some shut eye, for morning comes all too quickly, and we must see if we can make it down to the great Colorado River before sundown tomorrow? . . ."

Rugged terrain such as this the three Mexicans were traversing is especially breathtaking just before the sun's first rays come streaming over the hills to bathe the entire countryside in radiant light. A freshness is in the air, the same kind of freshness that must have greeted earth at the time the very first

107

rays of golden light broke through the dense cloud cover on the day of creation. Standing and imbibing the fresh, exhilarating morning air as the mournful pleadings of a dove broke the hushed silence, Sanchez was taken by the serenity of the moment. Meanwhile, their horses, mules, and one remaining burro were cropping grass contentedly, all of them looking rested after a night's repose.

Finally, their humble breakfast over, they again were on their way, their mission leading them unerringly toward Grand Bench, which lay on the west side of the river. Marveling at the terrain with its phantasmagorical sandstone forms, no two of them alike, they carefully picked their way toward the river. Suddenly ahead of them by no more than a hundred yards and moving in their direction, a small band of Navajos, each man wearing a large black uncreased hat, reigned in their horses. Surprised at seeing the approaching Mexicans, they waited until the latter had arrived within speaking distance. Sanchez, raising his hand in a gesture of friendship, smiled and said, "Good morning, gentlemen! Can you tell us roughly how far from the river we are?"

"The San Juan River," one of the Indians said pointing, "is about a half mile north of here. Some eight or ten miles west of here it empties into the Colorado."

"Good," Sanchez said, again smiling. "Our destination for the day is the river. Do you suppose we might be able to find someone there with a boat to transport part of our gear across the river? For one thing, we have a very large block of blue cheese that we've transported all the way from our hometown of Ascension, Northern Mexico, to present as a special and unexpected treat to some of our friends, all of them coal miners over in the Buckskin Mountains. And, of course, we mustn't risk getting this huge block of cheese wet, for that would spoil it."

"It's possible," the Navajo said. "Just this morning a large raft with several men and women floated by just after we had swum our horses across. Usually a couple or three times a year we go up to Escalante to do some horse trading and to sell blankets, rugs, saddles, bridles, and jewelry. Lots of friendly people up in Escalante, and they always make us feel welcome.

They're all the time giving us fruit and vegetables from their gardens and an occasional loaf of homemade bread and a big pat of freshly churned butter to go along with it. This, let me tell you, is a hundred times better than bread spread with wagon grease that a feller named John Mack gave us one time! He'd been hittin the bottle, so we just had to look over it and take it as a joke. But we like to go up to Escalante 'cause we're always able to sell or trade our wares up there. One feller in particular, a sheepman by the name of Shirts, always has horses to trade us for rugs and blankets. Course, his wife makes sure that she selects the rugs! She must have twenty of 'em by now. This Mr. Shirts is an unusual fellow. He always has at least one horse that he just wants to give us, but we don't do business that way. We always insist that he take however many rugs or blankets the horse is worth."

"That's all very interesting," Sanchez said. "It's a pleasure to meet you gentlemen. Some days ago we met a wonderful group of men from your tribe. We, unfortunately, didn't learn their names other than those of three young men, apparently their sons, who had gotten into trouble. Their names were Thomas, Johnny, and Owl Face."

Hearing these names, all of the Navajos started laughing. "Yes," their spokesman said, "you don't have to say more. Those three young men are always in trouble of some kind or another. What mischief one of them can't think of, the other two can!"

"Anyway," Sanchez said, "we were pleased to share half of a freshly killed deer with them, and then they overwhelmed us about an hour later by giving us a 100-pound sack of flour, which was a godsend because the last of our flour had run out about a week before. By the way, gentlemen, we'd be honored to give you a bag of buckmeat jerky if you'd care to have some to munch on as you ride back home."

His face lighting up immediately, the Navajo spokesman said, "You won't have to twist our arms on this one. Yes, we'll be pleased to accept your generous offer."

When Sanchez handed a bag of jerky to the Navajos, they reciprocated by giving each of the Mexicans a beautiful turquoise ring. "My goodness, gentlemen," Sanchez said, "this is overwhelming. We didn't expect you to give us anything in return. We simply have enjoyed meeting you fellows and passing the time of day with you. But thank you ever so much. We'll always treasure these rings." Julio and Jose also expressed their appreciation for this gesture of friendship.

In parting, the Navajos drew attention to a wonderful spring of cold water flowing out from under a rock ledge about three quarters of a mile west. "And at that same spot," the spokesman added, "you'll find some of the most succulent water kress you've ever eaten!"

"We can hardly wait. Thank you so much, gentlemen," Sanchez said as he and his partners were waving goodbye. . . .

Their waterbags virtually depleted, they welcomed with opened arms the glorious spring, whose refreshing waters would have equaled the sparkling water that Moses, empowered of Jehovah, drew from the rock when touching it with his staff. Drinking to their hearts' content and then watering their thirsty animals, slowly and in small amounts so as not to water founder any of them, they sojourned a good hour beside the spring as they munched on water kress and intermittently drank the water. "The ambrosia of the Olympian gods could not taste better than this," Julio commented while smiling ear to ear.

When fully refreshed and restored in both body and spirit, their animals likewise, the party proceeded on their way toward the mighty Colorado, the crosing of which would represent possibly their last really big hurdle before reaching their destination. The last mile or so they paralleled the San Juan down to its confluence with the Colorado. Spectacular Rainbow Bridge loomed large and majestic in the distance while the huge, halfmoon-shaped Navajo Mountain to the left was practically close enough to touch. Knowing that they simply couldn't risk taking the crate containing El Nino across the river other than by boat, they scoured the waters till after dusk, which time served as another welcome respite for their animals. Not knowing whether they would be forced to wait there for days or even weeks, they continued to scour the mighty river, whose surface at that point seemed so very serene. Yet they had heard that underneath its surface it was often like a veritable maelstrom, for once a person or an animal was swept under and caught firmly in the massive undertow, the result was frequently tragic. So they were forced to wait until a boat came along, but none came that day. After staking out their animals in a grassy area near the banks of the river, they made a fire and prepared their humble meal, remembering to look up and say thanks for all they had, especially for the precious drinking water. Again the stars came out in their glory, the vast Milky Way stretching obliquely across the heavens and teasing them with thoughts of other worlds out there in celestial space. In the distance coyotes could be heard howling and yowling, for this was the time of year for the females to be in heat. Their howling and yelping love songs continued for much of the night, but the men didn't fear those wild cousins of the domestic dog. For the time being the coyotes were thinking of something other than vittles. . . .

Morning came early, its freshness and beauty rivaling the same characteristics that must have typified the day of creation. Arising and preparing breakfast, which they ate slowly yet nervously, they scanned the river. Suddenly standing up and squinting, Jose exclaimed, "I think I see a boat coming around the bend in the river!" And sure enough, it **was** a boat. The three men, hastening down to the water's edge, waited expectantly until the man in the boat saw them. All three men motioning vigorously for the fellow to guide his boat over to the shore, they were gratified when he complied. Some twenty-five or thirty yards from the shore he called out, "What do you want?"

"Sir," Sanchez said, "we have a precious object weighing some fifty pounds that needs to be transported over to the west side of the river. We'll be happy to pay you for taking it over for us. It's a large block of blue cheese that we've transported all the way from northern Mexico, and we naturally can't risk getting it wet, for that would cause it to spoil.

Thinking about it for a moment, the fellow said, "Oh, all right. But I came here to fish and to sightsee, not to be anyone's taxi for hauling things across the river." They were gratified when the man approached the shore. In Spanish, Sanchez said

111

to his friends, "stand right here and keep an eye on us as we proceed across the river. Be prepared with loaded rifles just in case this guy should try something unexpected. Removing from his wallet one of the several $10 bills that Padre de Escalante had given him, Sanchez handed it to the man and said, "This should compensate you well for transporting this big block of cheese across the river for us. " Julio and Jose, carrying the crate with El Nino, gently loaded it into the boat, placing it midway between bow and stern. "I'll ride over with you, Sir," Sanchez said, "so that I can see that this precious cargo makes it dry shod over the waters, reminiscent of the ancient Israelites crossing dry shod through the Red Sea. We, of course, are going to cross over, not through, the water!" he said laughing. The proprietor of the boat merely eyed him suspiciously without saying anything. "And one other thing, Sir," he said, "do you think we also could transport a partial sack of flour over with this crate of cheese? The flour, as you know, would be ruined, too, if it should get wet in crossing."

"Oh, I suppose so," the man said after a moment's hesitation, "but for hell's sake don't ask me to take anything else. This is not a large boat; it can hold only so much."

"This will be the extent of what we need transported to the other side," Sanchez said, smiling and maintaining an upbeat attitude despite the unfriendly reception he was getting from the boatman Then turning to Julio and Jose, he said in Spanish. "Remember how we've talked about packing all of our goods as high as possible on the horses, the stirrups tied up over the packs for added stability. And, one other thing, Amigos. Have your rifles at the ready in case this hombre should try something unexpected during the crossing."

"Sure thing, Sanchez," Julio said.

Sanchez seated himself in the middle of the boat, his legs encompassing the crate with El Nino. The boatman, sitting on the seat behind him, manned the oars. Trying to make conversation since the man himself said nothing, Sanchez commented that the weather seemed ideal for crossing the river. "Is the water usually this calm?" he asked.

The surly boatman didn't answer, so Sanchez, still remaining upbeat, said, "Do you see many water fowl along the river these days?"

"You talk too much, feller," the boatman said. Then after a moment or two, they now being almost halfway across the river, he said, "So you say you have cheese in that crate, do you?"

"That's right," Sanchez said. "We've transported it all the way from Northern Mexico as a special treat for some of our coal-mining friends over west of here in the Buckskin Mountains. They hinted that we bring them a big block of cheese, but I'm sure they didn't think we'd actually do such a thing. It'll be interesting to see their expressions when they discover that we've brought this block of cheese along!"

"Are you sure that it's cheese you have in the crate, feller?" the boatman asked.

"Dead sure," Sanchez said, his blood pressure rising slightly at this yahoo's insolence. "Dead sure, for I helped pack it myself."

"Is that so?" the boatman said in a sneering tone.

"Si, padron," Sanchez said, "that **is** so. And what the hell does it matter to you what might be in this crate? For all you know, it might be filled with gravel or even dynamite, but that's none of your business whatsoever. You already have in your little grubby hands the $10 that I just gave you, so stop the sarcasm and just keep rowing if you know what's good for you. And for your own safety, you belligerent bastard, if you should be so stupid as to try something, my two partners right over there are crack shots with a rifle, and both are standing rifle in hand ready to plug you right between the horns if I should give the signal."

"Why, you impudent peon," the boatman said, face red with anger, "I ought to lambaste you right over the head with this paddle. No stinkin Mexican talks like that to me and gits away with it."

"I just did, mouse brain," Sanchez replied while turning around to face his opponent, "and as yet I haven't started shivering in my boots because of you."

113

Livid by now, the boatman managed to control himself long enough to try a little stratagem. "While you're running off at the mouth, you son of a buck," he said, you've placed too much weight on this end of the boat. Turn back around the way you were so you in your stupidity don't capsize us."

Finally complying, Sanchez stood up to turn around, but just as his back was turned momentarily to the boatman, the latter rammed him between the shoulders with an oar and knocked him into the water. "There, you smart-mouthed son of a buck," the boatman said as he stood up and slammed the paddle with tremendous force onto Sanchez's head, dazing him as he was trying to get back into the boat. Just then two rifle shots rang out simultaneously, one of the powerful slugs passing through the boatman's head, the other though his upper body and knocking him almost out of the boat. Sanchez clung to the boat for several minutes until he had recovered sufficiently from the blow with the paddle before climbing back into the boat. Pulling the now lifeless body of the boatman into the center of the boat, he proceeded to row toward the western shore, which was totally devoid of people. Other than Julio and Jose, no one had witnessed this incident. By this time they had started their animals across the river, each man grasping his horse's tail to be pulled safely to the west side of the river. Meanwhile, Sanchez, finally reaching the shore, rowed the boat up into a little shallow inlet and unloaded the crate containing El Nino, followed by the partial sack of flour that the friendly Navajos had given them. Then finding a rock weighing forty or so pounds, he carried it to the boat and, finding a length of rope lying in the bow, he used the same to tie the rock securely to the lifeless body. Removing the $10 from the man's pocket, he then rowed out about a third of the way into the river and dumped the body with the large rock attached and saw that cantankerous piece of human flesh disappear. "I've always taken a pragmatic approach to life's vicissitudes," he said half under his breath, adding, "I'll do all that's within my power to see that El Nino finds a temporary haven in one of those big caves on Grand Bench." Then he rowed back to shore, all the while scanning both sides of the

114

river as far as he could see in both directions. He and his two partners and their animals were the only living things in sight.

Presently Julio and Jose arrived with their animals, all of them, the little burro included, making it safely across. "Amigos," Sanchez said smiling, "that was one helluva performance by you two! That big brazen son of a buck clearly intended to knock me unconscious and let me drown. I'm beholden to both of you for saving my life."

"Sanchez," Julio said, unable to suppress a chuckle, "don't mention it. We know that if the tables had been turned, you would have done the very same thing for us. We're just grateful that all of us, El Nino included, made it safely across."

Finding a good place to dry off and let the animals rest, they themselves sought some welcome shade provided by one of many large cottonwood trees lining the west bank of the river. There they remained the rest of the day. But before they had settled down too comfortably, Sanchez took an ax and chopped a hole in the bottom of the boat, then set the craft adrift in the river, where it hadn't gone more than seventy-five yards before filling up with water and disappearing into the depths of the river. All traces of the unfortunate incident were buried forever in the river; and so far as they knew, the river wasn't talking. . . .

GRAND BENCH

The next morning after a satisfying breakfast of roasted bass, thanks to Jose, who had felt inspired to get up just before sunrise to try his hand at fishing, the party packed their animals and headed west up through a narrow canyon that took them out onto a juniper-bedecked plateau that they assumed must be the extreme southeastern end of Grand Bench. More or less due west lay the Buckskin Mountains, where the phantom coal miners would be awaiting their promised "blue cheese"! To be expected, they found the terrain for the first while rough and rugged. Since Grand Bench proper lay to the northwest, they nosed their way in that direction, all the while looking for any telltale signs of caves. They were not disappointed in their quest, for after a day's travel, they saw off in the distance somewhat west of northwest what appeared to be caves, from this distance little more than black holes dotting a sandstone ledge jutting out in the midst of the ubiquitous junipers.

"Can those be caves up in the distance?" Julio asked, shading his eyes against the glare of the afternoon sun.

"Yes," Sanchez said, unable to conceal his excitement. "Yes, if I'm not mistaken, those definitely are caves. But whether or not one of those is our definitive destination remains to be seen. So let's keep heading in that direction."

Traversing another big juniper-bedecked plateau rising gradually toward the north, they came ever closer to the caves, for they **were** caves. "I feel my heart beating a bit faster," Sanchez commented. "Does the sight and proximity of these caves do anything for you guys?"

"Yes," Jose said. "I feel a kind of quickening within me. But it's too late today to take a look at them, don't you think?"

"Right," Sanchez said resignedly. "Let's find us a suitable place to bed down for the night, a place where there's enough grass for these animals to make a meal out of. Then bright and early in the morning after grabbing us a quick bite to eat, we can go do some exploring."

"It looks as if we have the whole place to ourselves," Julio observed. "Would be awkward if other people should be passing through these parts."

"That's possible of course," Sanchez noted, "but not too likely. . . ."

After selecting a place to spend the night, they walked around a 100-foot radius of the place to check for rattlesnakes, this being a favorite place for the very dangerous diamond-backed rattler, and neither of them relished the thought of tangling with any of those treacherous beasts. Finding none of the slithering devils in their chosen area, they staked out their animals and said a few kind words to them, then bedded down nearby for the night. Having traveled so long and so far under often trying circumstances, they slept fitfully, all of them waking intermittently to contemplate where they actually were.

At about midnight Julio felt such a sudden rush of adrenaline that he had to get up for a while and walk around the perimeter of their encampment breathing deeply to try to calm himself. In the distance some coyotes were paying their respects to the moon, whose silver sheen had transformed the entire landscape, causing him to marvel at the stark beauty of the place. Off to the southeast and on the other side of the river he could see big Navajo Mountain standing boldly and proudly as if holding concourse with the Kaiparowits, or simply the Fifty-mile Mountain as Escalante's cowpokes referred to it. A gentle breeze caressing Julio's face, he found himself thinking that the Master Painter/Sculptor held everyone and everything in His hands. "But why is it," he mused, "that nature, especially during these hours of repose, can be so very lovely and peaceful while all too many people, the so-called zenith of divine creation, have to be so wicked and unkind to one another?" The incident involving the man in the boat was troubling to him. Besides sheer racial prejudice and perhaps greed, what exactly might have motivated the fellow to act so stupidly and unreasonably, leaving them no choice but to dispatch him prematuraly into the next world? "After all, our mission," he found himself verbalizing, "is of such magnitude that we simply can't let anyone or anything stand between us and the successful conclusion of the same."

A night bird sounded in the distance as two bats continued to patrol the area looking for flies and mosquitoes that might be hanging around till the last aromas of the men's humble meal had dissipated. A shooting star traversed a third of the sky, perhaps to bring the three devoted men good luck in their faithful endeavor. In a packbag next to the two sleeping men was the crate containing El Nino, a curious and inexplicable phenomenon. How long would El Nino repose in one of these caves? And how would this incomparable creation of gold find its way back to the Cathedral of the Blessed Virgin? These, of course, were questions that Julio simply couldn't answer. But within him welled up a sense of satisfaction that he, for all intents a nonentity, a man who had made no particular mark on the world, had been privileged to assist his close friends Sanchez and Jose in transporting El Nino all the way from northern Mexico up to Grand Bench in southeastern Utah. . . .

A holy hush seemed to pervade the air during those serene moments just before the first rays of the sun came streaming over the landscape. Awake and eager to be about their duties, the three men arose, stretched, breathed deeply, and set about preparing breakfast. Their meager domestic chores soon out of the way, they moved their animals up near the entrances to several caves. Thanks to some spring rains, a small stand of grass would keep the animals occupied while the men, after carefully surveying the area in all directions to see that they were alone, unloaded the crate containing El Nino and concealed the same by covering it with sagebrush. Then taking a shovel with them, they climbed up to the nearest cave to examine it and see if it might be a suitable place for hiding their precious cargo. Large enough to accommodate six or eight people, its walls were smoky, indicating that someone, perhaps Navajos many years ago, had lit a fire there. The exceptionally dry and fine sand on the floor appeared to be two or three feet deep. Looking at one another, the men finally shook their heads. "No," Sanchez said reflectively, "this doesn't impress me as the place we're looking for. Let's investigate some of the other caves."

The next cave, perhaps fifteen or twenty feet to the west, was not quite so large. Unlike the first, however, it had a number of petroglyphs on its walls. The thickness of the sand on the floor was about the same as that of the first cave. Again the men concluded that this was not the place for El Nino. So moving on to the third cave, which turned out to be about the same dimensions as the first, they again paused to study the petroglyphs, one scene depicting a hunter, bow and arrow at the ready as he stalked a deer. They were impressed with this cave, but not to the extent of concealing El Nino within its confines.

With similar results they inspected several more caves, some larger, some smaller than the others, but none of them apparently suitable for El Nino. Proceeding on to the next cave, which necessitated their climbing about thirty feet to reach its entrance, they were about to step inside when suddenly a cougar that had been nursing two kittens let out a blood-curdling scream and sprang to the entrance as if she would eat them alive! All three men, terribly shocked at this unexpected turn of events, practically fell all over one another in an effort to get away. As they hastily retreated down the steep incline, half running, half rolling, the jealous and protective mother stood just outside the entrance to her lair and growled threateningly, all the while baring her razor-sharp teeth and flexing her front claws. A veritable killing machine, she fortunately held her ground, satisfied that the intruders no longer were a threat to her babies. As for the three men, primordial fear had taken possession of them momentarily. Collecting their wits, they kept their eyes on the cougar as she stood guard above. Wisdom dictated that they take a wide berth around the next several caves, for they were careful not to intimidate the big cat any further. Sanchez, not wanting to risk losing any of their animals, asked Jose to return to guard them just in case the cougar decided to come and investigate.

The two men, continuing to explore more of the caves dotting the hillside to the west, came across a somewhat larger one that appeared to have had some help beyond that of Mother Nature, for the cavity was not round but almost square. Petroglyphs lined the west and east walls, but on the north wall was an unmistakable Roman cross. Its approximate age neither man was competent to say, but as laymen they concluded that it must have been there for a thousand years or more. After they had studied it for a while in silence, Sanchez said, "But how, pray tell, could anyone here on this continent and back in those days have known anything about a cross, a Roman cross at that? Surely there can't have been any Christians in these parts way back then!"

"We can only assume there were no Christians here a thousand or so years ago," Julio commented. Then tapping the floor with a shovel, he said, "Sanchez, I can't explain it, but I have the impression that we ought to see just how deep this sand is. Chances are that we might come across some very interesting artifacts. What d'ya say?"

"I'm inclined to think you're right," Sanchez said.

So they proceeded to dig. Down two feet they had found nothing, but the sand, though quite firm, could still be broken by a shovel. Down three feet they discovered a large, perfectly formed spearhead and several arrowheads, all of flint. Marveling at these unusual finds, they kept digging, trading one another off at intervals. Suddenly the shovel blade contacted a solid object, so carefully removing the sand from out around it, they were greatly intrigued to find three bowls and two vases of varying sizes and a grinding stone that had been used to grind corn into meal. Carefully removing the sand from the largest bowl, they were astounded to find two ears of typical "Indian" corn therein, the kernels slightly shrunk but otherwise intact and each of a different color, the dry sand having preserved them for lo these many years, perhaps for hundreds of years. The kernels of both ears appeared to be firmly attached to the cobs. Laying the two ears of corn down gently, they proceeded to remove the sand from the other two vases. With most of it removed from the larger of the two, Sanchez could feel a solid pointed object. Excitedly working it loose and withdrawing it from the vase, he dusted it off and held it in his hand. He and Julio looked at the curious object, then at one another, then back at the object. Both of them took a deep breath or two before either could speak. What they had found was a six-sided gold star of David, its luster not having diminished in all those centuries; for, unlike silver, gold doesn't tarnish. There it was, an actual six-sided star of David---two intertwined triangles, the one pointing down, the other pointing up to symbolize heaven reaching down and joining hands with earth!

"But **how**," Julio asked in disbelief, "could a star of David have found its way over to this continent?"

For several moments both men were speechless. Then Sanchez said, "How foolish and how very ignorant we mortals are! Can there have been Christians and even Jews here on this continent? There must have been! Otherwise who on earth would have drawn this Roman cross? And who would have deposited this star of David in this vase, obviously thinking that these artifacts eventually would be discovered?"

"I'll run back to relieve Jose," Julio said, "so he can come and see what we've found."

Minutes later Jose, quite out of breath, entered the cave. "Jose," Sanchez said ecstatically, "look at the treasure trove we've chanced upon!"

With a look of sheer disbelief, Jose picked up the bright star of David and studied it from all angles, noting the curious workmanship. Shaking his head, he said, "How can it be, Sanchez? How can it be? We know it is, and there's no denying it. But how did it get **here**?"

"Your guess is as good as mine, Amigo," Sanchez said, a slight smile stealing over his face. "But who will believe us even if we take this star of David back to Mexico and put it on display?"

"Yes, I see the point," Jose agreed resignedly. "But whatever else others may think, the three of us **know** what we've seen and where we have seen it. . . ."

Taking a brief time out for lunch, the three men moved their animals as close as possible to the cave and continued their excavation, additional artifacts such as bowls, vases, grinding stones, arrowheads and the like being discovered. Digging even deeper, they found nothing more. As for using this particular cave as the hiding place for El Nino, they decided against it. The Roman cross, they agreed, would be too much of a give-away.

So they continued to explore more of the caves until long about mid-afternoon when they entered one that seemed to have a particular ambience about it. Of average size and with a few petroglyphs adorning its walls, it seemed to have nothing of a physical nature that set it apart from any of the others; and yet, whatever it was about this cave, they knew intuitively that this was the one. Of this the three were at a unity of the faith. But just how, they mused, should they go about concealing El Nino here?

After a few moments of reflection, Sanchez said, "Amigos, a thought just came to me. Let's remove the sand here from the west side of the cave and then make an excavation into the west wall, carefully removing any of the sandstone chips from our excavation. Then after sliding the crate with El Nino into the recessed area, we can plaster up the entrance of the niche and doctor it up to look as if the spot had never been touched by human hands. Once we're satisfied with its appearance, we then can replace the sand to make it look as if no one had ever disturbed its long-lasting serenity. What d'ya say to this notion?"

"I believe you've just solved the problem for us," Julio said.

"I, too, believe you've hit upon the solution, Sanchez," Jose confided. "I suppose the thing to do now is to start shoveling sand over here to this side. By the way, how deep do you think we should dig?"

"Oh, I'd guess about five feet," Sanchez said. "What do you guys think?"

"Sounds about right," Julio said. . . .

The excavation took them a couple hours, after which they made a remarkable discovery. The west wall down at a depth of five feet was not solid sandstone as they had anticipated; it was sand of the same consistency as that they had been excavating. "Wow, does this ever solve one great big problem for us!" Julio said smiling. "I was dreading having to chip out a niche in the sandstone when our only tools are a pick and a shovel. This could lead one to believe that the Creator had prepared this cave for this particular purpose! But whether or not He did, we're grateful that we don't have to excavate through solid sandstone with a mere pick and shovel. We'd have been here a good long time accomplishing such a feat."

They carved the crypt about a foot deeper into the wall than the width of the crate containing El Nino. In the event that someone should remove the sand from this cave, the sand concealing El Nino very likely would not crumble to reveal the crypt. This, at least, was their thinking. And now, the crypt being prepared to receive its treasure, Julio and Jose carried the precious cargo up to the cave and handed it down to Sanchez, who set the crate down carefully, then positioned himself with his back against the east wall and his feet squarely against the crate. Carefully he pushed it into its new resting place. God alone, they mused, would know how long El Nino was to remain in this now sacred cave.

At this point Sanchez filled the opening of the crypt with sand, carefully tamping it into place and then proceeding to fill in the entire area with sand, which he likewise tamped together. His two partners each taking a turn, the floor of the cave soon was filled back up. Using one of their packbags, they removed the excess sand from the cave and distributed it in an area where it would look natural. Then demonstrating considerable skill and imagination, they scattered various bits of debris on the floor to make it look as if only animals and birds had frequented the place.

Returning to their animals, Sanchez said, "I don't know about the two of you, Amigos, but now that we've deposited El Nino in this temporary resting place, I feel both relieved and sad after traveling this far with the sacred statue. We must note carefully the location of this specific cave, for we have no way of knowing whether we or someone else will be sent to retrieve El Nino. I trust that God will see us safely back home to Ascension so we can give Padre de Escalante a full account of our travels and tell him precisely where on Grand Bench El Nino is in 'seclusion.'"

After resting the night, the three faithful Mexicans took a long and solemn look at the "El Nino Cave," then embarked on their arduous journey home. For a while they said nothing as they followed the same trail back to the river. Finally Sanchez

124

spoke. "With reference to our recent theological discussion," he began, "we didn't reach any concrete conclusions as to the validity of the Nicene Creed and related matters. But whether God is an actual Person or the incomprehensible Essence suggested by the creed, one thing is certain---El Nino is endowed with a benign spiritual aura. We've been witnesses of this much too often to deny it, not that either of us would ever contemplate such an unreasonable thing."

The three Mexicans retraced their path to the river and swam their animals across, clinging to the tails of their horses to be pulled carefully across the treacherous water as if they had done it many times. Even though they had packed their few belongings as high on the mules' backs as possible, some of the items, notably their extra rifles, got wet. So once on the east side of the river, they let the animals rest and proceeded to clean their weapons, an arduous task, but they fortunately had come prepared with cleaning equipment and oil for that specific purpose. On their way back to Monument Valley, they again encountered some Navajos, who wondered if they had any rifles they might want to sell or trade.

"Yes, as a matter of fact we do," Sanchez said, "and we'll make you an offer you can't refuse."

"Let's hear your offer," one of the Navajos said.

"We're almost out of flour," Sanchez told them. "Do you have any corn meal you can trade us? For a hundred pounds of corn meal we'll give you a couple good rifles that we feel we can get along without. It's pretty hard to eat a rifle, but we certainly would like some good corn meal!"

Chuckling at this wry humor, the Navajos said they probably could come up with the corn meal, but first they wondered if they might see the rifles. Retrieving a couple of Winchester 30.30s from the pack on their little burro, Jose handed them to Sanchez, who demonstrated the smooth bolt-action movement of both weapons for the interested Indians. Then he said, "Jose, you've got a couple cartridges in your pocket, don't you?"

After Jose had produced the same, Sanchez said to the Navajos, "See that black rock way over yonder on the bluff there among that stand of junipers?" They nodded. "Jose, show these gentlemen how you can hit that rock from here."

All eyes were riveted on Jose as he put a cartridge in the chamber of one of the rifles, took careful aim, and fired, blasting the top of the rock off. The Navajos cheered, one of them stating, "Man good shot. Not wise to keep running when he say stop!" All of the Navajos laughed.

"Now, Julio," Sanchez said, "demonstrate for these gentlemen how nicely the other rifle works," whereupon Julio, putting a bullet in the chamber, took careful aim and blasted off more of the top of the same rock. The Indians were visibly impressed.

"You hunt deer and mountain sheep?" one of the men asked.

"Only when hunger forces us to," Julio said smiling.

"Deer and sheep," he said, "they don't stand chance round you fellers!" Then he and his partners all laughed.

More than eager to trade corn meal for the two rifles, the Navajos returned not just with one sack of meal but with two and insisted that the Mexicans take them in exchange for the rifles. In addition, they presented each of the Mexicans with a beautiful blanket their wives had made. Gratefully Sanchez and his partners accepted. This transaction now over, the three Mexicans bade the friendly Navajos goodbye and proceeded on their way again. But after a number of days of steady travel, taking them roughly halfway down into Arizona, they felt it wise to bear off to the west, remaining in the wilds as much as possible, for they didn't want to meet anyone if they could avoid it. Finally within about fifty miles of the Mexican border, they turned east into New Mexico, carefully wending their way to within about twenty miles of Columbus before crossing over into home territory and back to Ascension, their long odyssey finally over. Filled with excitement at the prospects of being home after successfully completing the difficult and life-threatening assignment, they first of all were greeted most cordially by Padre de Escalante, Padre Ernesto, and the boy Amado. The next day after they had had time to be reunited with their families, the three of them met with de Escalante and Ernesto to give a detailed accounting of their often harrowing journey and how

126

Providence had protected and guided them to the sacred cave up on Grand Bench, where they had concealed El Nino for the duration. Their return trip, they explained, was not without its touch-and-go encounters, too; and all of these they likewise touched upon as they carefully related their exploits to the two interested padres, who lavished them with praise for the remarkable faithfulness and perseverance the three men had demonstrated. In retrospect, the three men were able to see the humor in some of their trials and tribulations, but at the time these things were happening, it was quite a different matter.

"Sterling characters all of you," de Escalante told them. "Truly sterling characters. To be able to call you gentlemen our friends is a distinct privilege for Ernesto and me. God will shower you with blessings for what you have done. . . ."

RE-ENTER THE NAVAJOS

Spying dates back to time immemorial, and what the three Mexicans did not realize is that two Navajos---Pete Indian and Jimmy Three Horses---had followed them to see exactly where in the Buckskin Mountains they were going to mine coal. However, when the Mexicans veered off to the northwest at the point where they otherwise would have continued due west, the Indians were more interested than ever in following them to see exactly what they might be up to. They concluded also that the crate containing the "blue cheese" very likely contained something quite different, something conceivably of great value; and whatever it was, they aimed to find out. Thus, they observed the Mexicans at fairly close range all the while they were depositing El Nino in his temporary hiding place in the now sacred cave on Grand Bench.

Wisdom dictated that they allow the Mexicans sufficient time to cross the river, for they didn't want to risk getting shot at if the Mexicans had stopped just out of sight to view the cave just in case any interlopers might have been there to engage in some skullduggery. "Well, Pete," Jimmy Three Horses said with a chuckle, "what say we go take a look at what them fellers wuz a doin up there? We know they wuz a buryin something in that cave, and it wasn't blue cheese either!"

Laughing, Pete Indian said, "That's for sure. But what if it was explosives of some kind? If we go a snoopin round up there, we could git our danged fool heads blowed off."

"Well, now, I hadn't thought o' that."

"It jus now popped into my mind. Now do you think we oughta risk gittin blowed to smithereens, as the white man he say?"

Scratching his head and thinking for a moment, Jimmy said, "No, course I don't. But I wonder if we creep up there right careful like, makin sure we don't disturb nothin, if we at least could take a peek inside that cave?"

"I dunno," Pete said. "But I'll tell ya what. Why don't you slip up there while I keep watch? You kin sneak up there as quiet as a cat and not disturb even a grain o' sand."

Laughing, Jimmy said, "Pete, you're jus a bullshittin me, telling me how careful I kin be cuz you yourself are too chicken to go up and take a look."

"No, I aint. I aint a bullshittin ya a tall," Pete said, trying to keep a straight face. " It's jus that I know you can be more careful than I could. Now when you git up there and nothin has happened to ya, you jus motion for me to come up, and I'll come right up."

"Okay," Jimmy agreed, "but now if I git blowed up, it's gonna be up to you to tell the wife and kids exactly what happened to me."

"Well, course I'd do that. Hell, you know I'd do that without bein told to. But I have the feelin that we really don't need to worry 'bout splosives bein stored in there. I'm convinced that them fellers has hid something of great value in that cave; and the more I think about it, the more convinced I am that we ought to investigate."

"Great idea, Pete my friend," Jimmy said laughing. "Now that you all of a sudden have convinced yourself that it aint dangerous a tall, I'll jus wait right here while you mosey up there to have a peek!"

"Now, looky here, Jimmy," Pete said defensively. "You tricked me right into this."

"No, it wasn't me that tricked you. You tricked yourself into goin up there to have a look. So let's see ya do it now so's we don't waste any more time a wranglin over nothin."

Seeing himself forced into a corner, Pete took a couple deep breaths and said, "Oh, all right. Now when I git up there, if it looks harmless enough, I'll motion for you to come on up and have a look, too."

"I'm your man," Jimmy said with a chuckle. "I'm your man."

"By the way," Pete said, "do ya think I oughta take a gun with me jus in case somebody's watchin us?"

"Oh, hell, I spose ya could, Pete, but I don't think there's another mother's son within thirty miles o' here right now."

"Well, I'll take this gun jus in case." So Pete Indian, rifle in hand, timidly made his way up to the El Nino cave. Once on a level with the entrance, he stepped as if the ground was a giant crate of eggs; and watching from down below, Jimmy Three Horses couldn't hold back the laughter. "For hell sakes, Jimmy," Pete said in a gruff whisper, "don't git me off kelter with yer laughin. After all, this is dangerous business, and I don't want nobody havin to come here and pick pieces of me off this damned sagebrush." Turning back around, Pete edged his way to the entrance of the cave and ventured a peek inside. Suddenly he felt a strange buzzing and humming in his head, all kinds of weird sounds coming into his right ear and going out his left ear. Also suddenly overcome with dizziness, he instinctively looked down at the ground to get his bearings and noticed what appeared to be dozens of black widow spiders crawling up his legs. Dropping his rifle and letting out several loud oaths in Navajo, he started flailing at both legs with his hands to knock the vicious-looking creatures off his legs, but they just kept coming. Issuing a distress call the likes of which his pal Jimmy had never heard him make before, he turned to run down over the embankment but ended up rolling and tumbling end over end, finally coming to a stop, his mouth and tongue covered with dirt. "Quick, Jimmy," he yelled. "Git these sonsabitches off me! They're crawlin all over me!"

"What's crawlin all over you?" Jimmy Three Horses asked, wondering if Pete was putting on an act of some kind.

"Why, these sonsabitch'n black widows! Hurry 'fore they eat me alive!"

"What on earth's come over you anyway, Pete?" Jimmy asked with alarm. "Have you lost your mind? There aint no damned spiders of any kind on you? What 'n the hell are you a tryin to scare me like this for? What's got into you anyway?"

"These spiders!" Pete yelled. "Quick! Don't jus stand there. Git these bastards off me!"

"Pete!" Jimmy yelled. "Git hold o' yourself. You're outa yer head. Why, hell, there aint no damned spiders of any kind on you. Take a look and see for yourself."

Timidly looking down at his legs, Pete, still sprawled on the ground, examined his legs and, to his unspeakable relief, saw that no spiders were crawling on him. Sweat pouring off his face, he said, "Jimmy, that wuz the awfullest experience I ever had in all my born days. I swear I wuz covered with black widows when I came rollin and tumblin down that slope. I seed 'em. They wuz all over me. And my ears are still ringin with all kinds o' strange noises like I aint never heard before."

"Well, stand up, Pete," Jimmy said, now inclined to believe that what Pete had been saying was real. "Maybe if ya stand up you'll feel better."

Trying to stand up, Pete said, "Why , hell, man, I can't even git up. The earth's turnin round and round. Grab me, Jimmy, so I don't fall off!"

Almost laughing at this last remark, Jimmy reassured his friend that the earth wasn't turning wildly and that there were no spiders crawling all over him. "Jus lay there for a few minutes, Pete," he said, "and maybe you'll feel better. What in the world happened to you up there anyway? You even left your gun up there. One of us will have to go up and git it."

"Well, **I** sure as hell aint goin back up to that sombitch'n place no more. I learned my lesson. A herd o' wild horses couldn't git me back up there no more. And if you don't believe me, Jimmy, jus go up there and see for yourself. That 'll make a believer outa ya right fast. Go on! Go up and see for yourself!"

"Now, Pete, let's be realistic. We can't go off and just leave your gun up there."

"Try me. To hell with that gun. I aint goin back up there, Jimmy, and that's that. If you're so fond of that gun, then **you** go up there and git it."

"All right, Pete, I will. We can't just take off and leave your gun up there."

"Fine, Jimmy boy. Now this I want to see. I kin rouse myself enough to set up and watch this great demonstration you're gonna put on for us."

132

"Pete, you sound like you'd lost all yer marbles. I didn't say I wuz gonna go up there and look directly into the cave itself. I jus said I wuz gonna go up there and fetch yer rifle back."

"Great. March right up there. This I wanna see."

Jimmy Three Horses, understandably somewhat fearful as a result of what he had just observed in Pete, proceeded up the incline leading to the cave. Once on the level with the entrance, he saw the rifle lying there in the dirt and bent down to pick it up. As soon as he touched it, there was an exceedingly bright flash and an ear-splitting clap of thunder, knocking him to the ground, which he discovered to be vibrating as if an earthquake would occur at any moment. Intuition told him to lie right still for the time being till he could get his bearings.

"What happened, Jimmy?" Pete called out in alarm when he saw his friend knocked violently to the ground although he had seen no light and heard no clap of thunder. "You all right, Jimmy? You all right?" Getting no response, he decided to stand up and discovered that he could. Amazingly, his dizziness was gone and the buzzing and humming in his head had faded away almost entirely. "Jimmy!" he yelled. "Jimmy! You all right?" Still getting no response, he walked partway up the incline and called out again. "Jimmy, you all right?" No response. Cautiously climbing up a few feet higher, he called out in not much more than a gruff whisper, for he didn't want to disturb the gods or the witches, goblins, spirits, or whoever or whatever was responsible for these strange reactions. "Jimmy, you all right?"

Finally he noted a slight bit of movement; and Jimmy, voice barely audible, said, "Pete, I seem paralyzed. I can't move a muscle."

"Jus lay there a moment or two until your body recovers from the shock," Pete advised. "I don't know exactly what happened to you, but you don't have to try to prove to me that something **did** happen to you. Jus lay there a minute; but, for hell's sake, don't touch that gun again!"

"Don't touch that gun again?! That thing's got 'lectricity or sompin like that in it. Nobody or nothin could git me to ever touch that thing again."

133

"What'd I tell ya jus 'fore you climbed up there?" Pete said. "I told you that gun wasn't worth it. Now whatever you do, **DON'T look inside that cave!**" Are you feelin any better now?"

"Yes, I'm a little better. But I'm havin a hard time seein, and I'm bleedin. There's blood all over my face, and I don't know where all else. It feels like I'm bleedin all over."

"Well, see if you kin crawl over here toward me," Pete suggested. Crawl right over here so I kin git hold of your hands. Then I'll pull you down over the edge."

With considerable effort Jimmy managed to crawl over to the edge and extend a hand to his friend. But the instant that Pete touched his hand, a violent surge of energy and heat entered his body, momentarily paralyzing his hand and arm. Reacting normally, he tried to let go but couldn't. Gradually, however, the energy or whatever it was subsided, and he pulled his friend over the edge, from where both of them rolled and tumbled down to the bottom and came to rest against a large juniper.

Gaining control of himself, Pete was astounded when he looked at his friend. "Jimmy!" he exclaimed. "Jimmy! Why, hell, you're a bleedin from every hole in yer head---from your eyes and ears, from yer nose and mouth. Are you okay, man?"

"I'm feeling jus a bit better, Pete." he whispered, "but I'm havin a helluva time seein."

"I guess you are! Why, your eyes are all bloodshot; blood's dripping out of both sides of 'em."

"**That** wuz a shock, Pete, like I didn't even know existed," a still rattled Jimmy Three Horses said feebly. "Let's jus lay here a while longer till I kin unrattled and git back on my feet. Right at the moment I can't even git up. I know I can't. There's no use even tryin. If a big diamond-backed rattler wuz comin at me right now, I couldn't even move. I'd jus have to lay right here and let the sombitch bite me."

"Lay right still for a minute or two, Jimmy," Pete said. "And forgit that gun."

"Forgit that gun, did you say?! Why, for all I care, that confounded thing can lay right up there till not so much as a rust spot's left of it. I wouldn't touch that old shooting iron again for all the horses in Utah and Arizona combined; and you kin toss in all the deer and jack rabbits to boot."

Gradually coming to themselves again, both men looked at one another in a way that said, "Let's git outa here pronto." And discovering that they could walk now although a bit unsteady on their feet, they carefully made their way down to where their horses were tied up. Apparently neither one of the horses had seen or heard anything out of the ordinary. . . .

And thus it was among the Navajos that the tale of the Sacred Cave originated and spread like wildfire throughout the land where **The People** dwelled. A few, particularly the young, naturally daring one another, sought to retrieve the rifle, but they were spared the shocking experience of actually touching it and having the equivalent of a few thousand volts pass through them. Sheer curiosity drew them to the environs of the cave, and from a safe distance they surveyed the exact spot. Several of the young bucks tempted one another to venture up to the cave entrance to grab the rifle and make off with it, or simply to steal a quick glance inside the cave. But each time they started up the embankment their strength somehow failed them; and try as they would, they couldn't get up to where Pete Indian's rifle lay in the dirt near the cave entrance.

One young brave said, "Watch me. I'm gonna start runnin and not stop till I kin see inside that cave." Taking off with all his might, he made it almost to the top of the incline when suddenly his feet seemed to turn to lead; then flailing his arms to catch his balance, he did what amounted to a backward somersault and came crashing end over end till he landed at the feet of his astonished and frightened friends, where he lay pale and totally enervated, his breathing uneven and labored. For several moments no one dared say anything or even move, each of them standing as if rooted to the ground.

Finally, one young lad, managing to unloose his tongue, said, "Tony, are you all right? Tony? You all right? Speak to us!"

Presently the much shaken youth's eyelids began to flutter slightly, indicating that he was coming to himself again. Sitting up moments later, eyes wild with fright, he said, "Let's git away from this gawd-dammed place! No one will ever have to tell me again that this is No Man's Land right here around these caves. There's sompin up there that we don't know nothin about and aint 'sposed to know nothin about."

This day's activities and a few isolated attempts the next two weeks proved to the Navajos that only someone exceptionally stupid would venture to make off with the now-infamous rifle or try to steal a glance into the cave. The general consensus among these folk was that the three Mexicans had deposited a very precious or sacred object of some kind therein. For a number months speculation ran wild as to what it was, and many members of the tribe, young and old alike, ventured to within thirty or forty yards of the place to have a look and to air their various opinions about the whole affair. But, of course, no one was in a position to confirm his respective hypothesis. In time little more was said about the cave except that only the addle-brained would try to enter it. . . .

THE ESCALANTE MEN

Savoring the sheer joy of riding his smart-stepping quarter horse bright and early in the morning, Chess Lay was passing Smith Alvey's place on the southeast edge of Escalante just as Smith came outside to change the water on his lawn.

"Morning, Chess!" Smith said smiling.

"Top o' the mornin to you, too, my friend!" came the cheerful reply.

"What happened anyway?" Smith said, eyes twinkling. "Did Ruth kick you outa bed this morning for misbehavin!"

"Hell, Smith," Chess said grinning broadly, his gold tooth sparkling in the morning sunshine, "when I raised up in bed and took a gander out the window just before the sun peaked over the hill, it wuz so damned purty outside that I told the wife I wuz gonna go saddle my horse and take a little spin around town. Besides, I thought I'd better go ride this testy sombitch and not give him any more oats for a while. A couple days ago when I got on him he lowered his head and humped up his back, and the next thing I knew I wuz pickin myself up outa the weeds. Hell, I musta sailed fifteen or twenty feet out through the toolies cuz a couple crows'd built a nest on me 'fore I landed! And that patch o' hard ground where I returned to earth I wouldn't exactly call a mattress!"

Laughing, Smith said, "Well, as I've told you before, Chess, you'll have to start clinging to the saddlehorn!"

"I'll sure keep that in mind the next time!"

"By the way, Chess, is there anything to that wild story about you being up to ol' Dagger Jack's the other night?"

"Yes, by thee wars, I'm afraid it's true," Chess said grinning. "And I wanna tell ya that that shindig wuz a hair raiser I don't plan to repeat for a while."

"Is it true that ol' Dagger Jack, with about three sheets to the wind, came at you with a butcher knife?"

"I'm afraid that's true, too."

"Well, I'll bet you didn't let much grass grow under your feet as you were exiting the premises!"

"Well, now, I don't know 'bout that, Smith. But one thing I **can** tell you for sure is that when I got home and wuz just reaching out to git hold of the doorknob, two gates fell off the front of me--one was ol' Dagger Jack's and the other wuz pa's!"

"That wuz some fast moving!" Smith said laughing heartily. Then abruptly changing the subject, he said, "Tell me, Chess, is there anything to this rumor I've been hearin about you and ol' Delane goin down on Grand Bench to find that statue of the gold Jesus?"

"That runor's right smack dab on the money, Smith," Chess said with an air of importance. "You know, all the while I wuz a growin up, my mother had a strip of buckskin with a map showin the location of that cave. I don't know what ever become o' that piece of buckskin, but I remember which one of them caves the map pointed to."

"Well, I suppose most people here in town have heard one thing and another about that map, but most of them tend to think it's just a wild story."

"No, it's not just a story, Smith, for I saw that map many a time while I wuz growin up. In fact, my mother promised it to me. You see, my stepgrandfather, Lewellen Harris---the wash just out south of town, you know, is named after him---anyway, Lewellen Harris spent quite a number of years as a self-proclaimed missionary to the Navajos. After a time they took him into their confidence and told him a number of things about some of their rituals and stuff that Navajos just don't tell white people. Hell, they even showed him one of the odd-looking sheepskin garments that they wore for special ceremonies. My granddad said it reminded him somewhat of Mormon temple garments. Then one day they decided to take him over onto Grand Bench and point that cave out to him. The only thing he had to draw a map on was a piece of buckskin, and that heirloom remained in our family for years. The Navvies, you know, were afraid to git too close to that cave. They thought there wuz some magical powers or the like associated with it, and I guess there must have been because my Grandfather Harris said a team of wild horses wouldn't a been enough to drag any one o' them Indians up to that cave. In fact, Smith, they told my granddad

138

that a 30.30 rifle that a member of their tribe had dropped right there in front of the cave is still a layin there. Now what d'ya think o' that?"

"Well, that's a purty wild story, Chess!" Smith said, chuckling amiably. "And so you and Delane are gonna go down there and prove to them Navvies that there's nothing to that magic business they still talk about. Is that right?"

"I hope to spit in yer mess kit if that aint right," Chess said merrily. "Yes, sir, that's what we're a fixin to do 'fore somebody else beats us to it."

"And what 're you gonna do with all that gold?" Smith asked in jest.

"Well, by thee wars, the first thing we're gonna do is melt that sombitch down!"

"Melt it down! Do you mean to tell me, Chess, that you'd melt down a valuable piece of art like that must be?"

"Why, hell, yes! If that Mexican Government got wind of us havin that statue, they'd contact our government and take it away from us. So the best thing to do is to melt it down as fast as possible and make gold bars out of it and tell everybody that we found us a little gold mine out there'n the Buckskin Mountains."

"So it sounds to me like you two fellers plan to git rich on this little venture!"

"Git rich? Why, I hope to shout in your ear that we plan to git rich! We're gonna be sittin purty. I'll see that the wife's all decked out in stardust and spangles!"

"Now, Chess," Smith said laughing. "you'd better not make too big a plans before you have them gold bars right in your hands."

"We'll have 'em in our hands, by golly. Yes, sir, we'll have 'em in our little grubbies for sure."

"And so what are you gonna do for yourself, Chess, with all that money?" Smith asked, again laughing.

"What am I gonna do for myself? **Why, I'm gonna be ridin a silver saddle**! That's what I'm a gonna be doin! . . ."

Continuing on his way, Chess swung up around his pal Delane Griffin's place and whistled. When Delane came to the door, Chess grinned and said, "Well, Delane, I kin see that you've been relishing your breakfast---you've got part of that fried egg on your collar!"

Glancing down at his collar and grinning, Delane said, "Oh, that's easy to explain, Chess. You see, just as Leah was gittin ready to put that egg on my plate, she tripped on the rug. I thought for a second she wuz gonna put both the egg and the spatula in my mouth at the same time! . . . Now do you have your bedroll ready and your grub box packed? And you didn't forgit **your own** favorite spatula, did ya?"

"Hell, no. I wouldn't forgit that spatula for the world. I give the wife strict instructions to put that dude in my grub box, so it'll be there. Yes, I'm all set to go. Now, d'ya wanna leave today or first thing in the morning?"

"Well, I spoke to Cecil, and he said he'd do my chores for me, so we might just as well take off this morning."

"We still goin in this old Ford pickup o' yourn, Delane?"

"I'm afraid so. That's all I've got at my disposal right at the moment."

"You bought this old bucket o' bolts from Charley Bailey, didn't you?"

"Ja, that's who I got it from."

"How much did this little transaction set ya back anyway?"

"Oh, I ended up givin ol' Charlie that sorrel mare and a cow for it."

"Well, I hate to say this, my friend, but I believe you got took! You gotta watch ol' Charlie. He's a wise old duck."

"Yes, that he is. But this old crate runs like a charm. Now, I wouldn't try to drive it up through Colletts 'cause I know it wouldn't make it. We'll have to head up the Wash and out past Big Sage and down that way to git to Grand Bench."

"The road down through there should be in purty good shape. It's only been a couple weeks since ol' Rodney Cottam run the grader all the way down through there and out into the Buckskin Mountains where them fellers is a drillin for oil."

"You got a good sharp ax and a pick, Chess?"

"Ja, got 'em both leanin against my grub box so I don't forgit 'em."

140

"Well, I've got a couple shovels we can take. And how 'bout Old Betsy, that old 25.35 of yourn? You're takin it along, aren't ya?"

"I sure as heck am, Delane. You never know what you might run into down in that wild country."

"I'm takin my 30.30 and plenty o' shells. Dependin on how long we end up staying there, we might just have to go and git us a little camp meat! There's some big bucks down in among them cedars."

"I'll say there is. Well, I'll take this horse on down home and meet you there in, say, half an hour."

"That's just about how long I need to throw my gear together and to git this egg off my collar! Then I'll be right down, Chess. . . ."

The weather was beautiful as the two gold diggers headed out past the old shearin krell, which had long fascinated all the kids in town, and on up into the mouth of the Alvey Wash.

"You know, Delane," Chess commented, "it doesn't matter how often I come up through this old wash, I still find it intriguing. All these hills up through here bear a lot of similarities, and yet no two of 'em are exactly alike."

"I'm the same way," Delane added. "I've always enjoyed comin up through here ever since I was a kid. Course, now, it's not a good place to be if it's stormy. Those big old floods that come a rip-snortin down through this canyon pick up everthing in their wake. Livestock, I can tell you, are smart enough not to git caught in one of these floods. Oh, that's not to say I haven't seen animals caught occasionally, but it's rare. Animals, you know, seem to have an added sense in this regard. They can tell if a flood's comin. They can smell it, and that gives 'em time to head for the high ground."

"Ja, that's true. Whenever we have one of them old big floods come roarin past our place down there, I still can't resist the temptation to mosey down to the crik bank and watch it. There's something wicked lookin about the way one o' them big walls of muddy water comes bullin its way a pushin trees, old wrecked cars, and whatever else gits in the way."

141

"Grand Bench," Delane commented, "is a bad place for flash floods. I've seen some humdingers down in that country."

"Yes, I have too," Chess said. "Good thing the weather's in our favor right now; otherwise I'd be a bit spooky about headin down into that neck o' the woods."

"Well, I frankly don't think we need to have any worries about the weather this trip," Delane noted. "It's been purty dry around this whole area for the past month."

"Yes, we'll git down there and find that cave and start diggin. Once we locate the statue, we'll grab it and git the hell outa there."

"How exactly do we know, Chess, that it's a gold statue? I've heard for years that that's what it's supposed to be, but I'm wondering how we can be sure."

"That's a good question. I can tell ya that none of them Navvies knows what's in the cave. All o' them fellers is superstitious about gittin too close to the place. They know which cave it is 'cause, as I mentioned the other day when we wuz talkin about it, they finally opened up to my grandfather, Lewellen Harris, and actually took him out by them caves and showed him which one the statue was in."

"So why didn't Harris walk up and investigate the cave?"

"Well, now, I don't know for sure, but I think the Navvies were afraid to let him climb up to it. They wuz all convinced that something terrible would happen to him if he even so much as looked inside the cave."

"So what you're sayin, Chess, is that the Navvies really don't know what's in there, but I've heard that some of them have been known to speak of a gold statue of Jesus bein hid there. What I'm wonderin about is just how they'd a come to that conclusion when neither one of 'em's been brave enough to go and investigate."

"The only thing that comes to mind is that some of 'em got wind of ol Pancho Villa's repeated attempts to make off with that gold statue of Jesus down there in Northern Mexico. Rumor has it that it was supposed to weigh about 50 pounds, which explains why Villa was so hellbent on stealing it from the

142

church. That old boy wanted to melt it down into gold bars so he'd have enough money to pay his troops."

"Now that you mention it, Chess, I do recall hearin something about that statue, too. Somehow---I don't know any of the details---somehow Villa never did manage to git hold of the statue, I'm told."

"That's right, Delane. Then one day that statue just come up missing and hasn't been seen since. Now this is the story, so far as I know, that the Navajos heard; and apparently they put two and two together and come up with the notion that what them three Mexicans hid in that cave was that very statue. And if that's what it turns out to be, my friend, we're gonna end up with it! Yes, sir, by gum, we're gonna end up with it, and it'll put both of us on easy street for the rest of our lives!"

Laughing, Delane said, "Well, that sounds purty good in theory at least. But what if it turns out that the cave **is** hexed? Do you think something like that's actually possible in this day and age, Chess?"

"Well, come to think of it, I suppose it is. I know for a fact that it was the old Devil himself that jumped down outa that big cottonwood tree there on the corner of Willard Heaps' place the night a bunch of us kids, all of us just big kids at the time, wuz a sittin there leanin up against that tree a talkin and foolin around. Before the old feller jumped outa the tree, sparks commenced to rain down on us; and 'bout the time we looked up, he landed right in the middle of us with sparks flyin everwhere. Now I **know** it wuz the old Devil himself 'cause I saw them big hairy ears, his pointed teeth, and his forked tail! The smell o' brimstone wuz so strong that we had it all over our clothes. And I wanna tell you that never in your life, Delane, have you ever seen kids scatter the way that old Feller scattered us. Ol Reed Wooley and them two boys o' Hen Heaps' wuz so scared that they jumped clear down over them big high crik banks and run on up through the fields over across the crik 'fore they got home."

Having a good laugh at all this, Delane said, "Now tell me, Chess, what exactly did **you** do when the Devil jumped outa that tree?"

"What did I do? Why, I musta broke two or three world records as I hightailed it right down the sidewalk past Lorenzo Griffin's place. In fact, I wuz movin so fast by then that before I could make a left turn to head down toward George Campbell's, I'd run clear across to the east side o' the street and got big slivers all up my right leg where I smoothed out ol John King's fence. Why, hell, the sparks wuz just a flyin as I went fullblast down that graveled road past George Campbell's and Frank Liston's. And as I went sailin through the intersection ol Hyme Bailey hollered out, 'Who the hell's after ya, Chess!' When I wuz almost home I took a big flying leap and sailed over our front gate just like I had wings and practically knocked the door down gittin in the house. It being summertime, my bed wuz out under them apple trees, but I wuz so scared that I rushed into ma and pa's bedroom and jumped right in bed with them with all my clothes on!"

"That's one helluva story, Chess!" Delane said laughing heartily. "So am I to understand that you believe what all o' them Navvies have been sayin about being afraid to go inside that cave?"

"Well, I guess I do and I don't."

"Now when we git down there, you're not gonna chicken out on me, are you, and refuse to go inside the cave?"

"No, I don't believe I will," Chess said grinning. "Hell, after we've come all this way, neither one of us can chicken out, can we?"

"Not if we're serious about makin off with that gold statue . . . ."

"You know, Delane, we're gittin clear out here to hell and gone. Give us 'bout another half hour and we'll be within throwin distance o' them caves. Say, do you see all that dust out there to the east?

"Yes, as a matter of fact I do. Looks like it might be a couple o' cars or trucks headin in our direction. Where d'ya spose they've been anyway?"

"I don't rightly know," Chess said, trying to figure the situation out. "Now, by thee wars, would you believe that somebody's followin us, too? Look back there. We might just as well stop right down here and have a convention!"

Minutes later the two pickups coming from the east were practically upon them, so they pulled over to the side o' the road and stopped. And no sooner had they stopped than the truck that had been following them also pulled over and stopped. The driver in the first pickup, pulling up alongside, said, "Say, are you men from around here? We're lost and need some direction."

"Well, that's nothing out of the ordinary," Chess said chuckling. "I suspect all of us need a little direction in life from time to time!"

Grinning at the wry humor, this fellow and his two partners started to get out of the pickup, so Delane and Chess followed suit. Then the men in the other two pickups also got out and came up to listen to what was being said.

"Well, now, to answer your question," Chess said, "we're both cowpokes from Escalante. My name's Lay, and this is my friend Delane Griffin. He runs his cattle right up here on the Kaiparowits," Chess said pointing. "And where are you fellers from?"

"We're all from Texas," the driver of the first pickup volunteered.

"All six of you from Texas?" Chess asked smiling.

"All six of us."

"Well, what on earth," Chess said, eyes twinkling, "would entice you fellers leave the Yellow Rose of Texas to come all the way up here into this god-forsaken country?"

"We're all geologists, and somebody told us about some caves in this general area, so we thought that since we had a little time on our hands we'd go and take a look at 'em 'fore headin home."

"I see," Chess said, rubbing his chin as if in thought.

Then Delane, turning to the men that had been following them, said, "And what about you fellers? Where you from?"

"California. Both of us from the Los Angeles area."

"Smiling, Delane said, "Well, you must be lost for sure. This is the end o' the world way out here."

145

Laughing, the one said, "We hope not! Our map actually shows this dirt road. You see, we're what they call speleologists—cave enthusiasts. We've visited caves all over the world, and we heard recently that there are some very interesting caves down here on Grand Bench."

"**Caves** you say?" Chess asked, pretending to be surprised. "**Caves** down here on Grand Bench?"

"We can't find any listed on this map, but we heard from a fairly reliable source in L.A. that some big caves are out in this general area. A dentist down there by the name of Lorrin Shurtz, originally from Escalante, told us about 'em. One cave in particular they say the Navajos refuse to go near. That intrigues us. We'd like to see what there is about the cave that would cause them to shy away from it."

"Oh, I see," Chess noted thoughtfully. "I might a heard something about that myself." Then pointing south, he said, "Now, there's some caves down there on the north side o' the Buckskin Mountains; they're a little ways out past where them fellers down there's a drillin for oil."

Then Delane, speaking up, said, "What you fellers 'll have to do is to continue west on this road for about eight or ten miles till you come to the cut-off that will take you down to the southeast. That road, recently graded 'bout the same time as this one, will take you right out into that country."

"Yes," Chess piped up, "and if you don't happen to see them caves, don't be discouraged. Just keep scourin them old hills there to the south and you'll find what you're a lookin for."

"Well, thanks a lot," the spokesman for the Texans said. "We'll go and give it a shot. By the way, we noticed that the mosquitos are bad down there close to the river. Is this typical of the area?"

"Oh, long 'bout this time o' year," Chess said, "they can git a little pesky at times down in that vicinity."

"Well, I suppose the saving grace," the Texan said, "is that they're a helluva lot smaller than the mosquitos down in Texas."

"You got some big ones down there, have you?" Chess asked. "Roughly how much bigger would you say they are, right off hand?"

146

"Shucks, I'd say they're at least twice or three times as big as these here."

"Well, now, let me tell you," Chess said with an air of authority, "if any of you fellers ever git out here on the Kaiparowits, you'll encounter mosquitos way BIGGER than that."

"BIGGER than those in Texas?" the Texan asked in disbelief. "My hell, man, just how much bigger could they be anyway?"

"Oh, I haven't actually gone to the trouble of measuring any of 'em," Chess commented, "but just to give you kind of a ballpark idea of their size, I saw one the other day stand flat-footed and climb a turkey!"

When all the others burst out in uproarious laughter, the Texan, finally joining in the fun, could see that he'd been put in his place.

"Anyway, fellers," Chess said, still smiling from the moment of levity, "as Delane here mentioned a moment ago, if you'll head west some eight or ten miles, you'll come to the cut-off that'll take you down into the Buckskin Mountains and out to them caves. There must be, oh, I'd say 'bout a dozen of 'em. Is that what you estimate their number to be, Delane?"

"Yes, I'd say that's a fair estimate," Delane said, maintaining a straight face.

"You two gentlemen," one of the Californians said, "appear to be headed out onto Grand Bench."

"Yes, that's where we have a little matter of business to tend to," Chess said.

"Business? Out on Grand Bench?"

"Yes, business of a sort. You see," Chess said, "I'm part Navajo. You can tell just by looking at my nose and these high cheekbones. And besides that, I'm bowlegged. You see, when my mother wuz a carryin me, she had occasion to spend most of her time out in this country astraddle a horse while herdin sheep. Anyway, my maternal grandmother, bless her kind old heart, was down in this area recently and forgot her purse. I say 'purse.' It wuz actually a sheepskin bag with a drawstring in it. She and my mother had been sittin up in one o' their favorite Moqui houses

147

down there in the lower ledges eatin pinenuts; and when they'd et their fill, they got up to leave, and grandma, without thinkin, walked off without her handbag. Not until they'd got almost up to Escalante did she happen to notice it gone. Alzheimers, you know, afflicts the Navajos, too! Anyway, she said, 'No cause for alarm. I'll just send ol Chess back down there to git it.' She's a wise old duck, my Navajo grandmother. She knew she wouldn't have to twist my arm to git me to go back down there and git her handbag 'cause she'd wrote out her will on a piece o' buckskin statin that I'm to inherit a thousand head of her best sheep, them that have the different-colored wool that the Navajos use to make their rugs and blankets out of. And that piece o' buckskin's in that leather bag. So that's our errand, gentlemen."

"What in the hell's a Moqui house?" one of the Texans asked.

"Oh, that's what all the locals around here call them Indian storage houses up in the ledges. Some of 'em have been there for a thousand years, I'd reckon."

"You're bound to see some of 'em," Delane added, "when you git down there in the Buckskin Mountains. Some of 'em in fact are so high up that it's doubtful if anyone's ever been in 'em since the Indians built 'em. I wouldn't recommend that you try to climb up to any of the higher ones; it's simply too dangerous. And that's no place to fall and break an arm or a leg."

"Yes, he's right," Chess said, eyes twinkling. "If that happens to anyone out in these parts, they usually just shoot him and leave him there 'cause it's too much bother to transport him out of a place like that!"

Well, after another good laugh, the party broke up. The two Escalantans wished the strangers good luck, bade them goodbye, and proceeded on their way out onto Grand Bench, their desired destination being about a thirty-minute drive from that point.

"Chess," Delane said laughing, "there's never a dull moment around you! 'They usually just shoot 'em,' huh?!"

"Well," Chess said with a chuckle, "I figured that wuz the best way to git 'em off our scent! Let's just hope they don't come back. If they do, Delane, I'll let you spin the next yarn!"

148

The little old Ford pickup kept putt-puttin right along; and hardly 'fore they knew it, they'd come to the place where they had to turn off the road and head north, making their own trail up through the junipers to the foot of the low ridge with the caves. "I wish there wuz some way we could a concealed our tracks," Chess commented. "If them fellers decide to come back, they sure as the world 'll see where we turned off; then they'll follow us to see what we're up to."

"There's no doubt in my mind," Delane said, "as to why all o' them fellers are out in this area. They've heard about that gold statue supposedly buried in one of these caves."

"Yes, what I'm worried about," Chess added, "is that we might see some fireworks 'fore this little expedition's over. I hope we git outa here without some unnecessary holes in our hide!"

When the motor started to lug down because of the steepness and the sandy terrain, Delane turned the pickup facing east and stopped. "It's better not to have either end of this contraption pointing downhill," he said with a chuckle. "I don't put too much trust in this emergency brake."

By now it was early afternoon, so the two men got out and stretched and decided to take a moment or two to have a bite to eat. "Well, Chess," Delane said, "what d'ya think? Which one of these caves should we try first?"

"I'd say that one right up there to the left o' that little ridge. It looks to me like the one indicated by the map on that piece o' buckskin ma had."

"You're not gonna be skittish on me now about goin into the cave, are you?" Delane asked smiling.

"Oh, no. Course, now, if what these Navvies have been saying turns out to be true, we might go up there and git the hell scared out of us!"

"Well, let's mosey up and take a look. We'll know for sure which cave it is because the rifle the one Navajo left up there should still be layin on the ground near the mouth of the cave."

Shovels in hand, they proceeded to climb up to the level of the cave entrance; and, sure enough, lying there fully exposed to the power of the sun was an old badly rusted-out rifle. "What d'ya think we oughta do with this gun?" Chess asked, actually feeling a bit skittish.

"Well, now, I'll tell ya," Delane said. "We'll just take it home as a souvenir. The townspeople 'll git a big kick outa seein something as famous as this. Quite a few of 'em have heard about this gun anyway and about how the Navvies dassn't come near it. We'll play this one up big!"

"You gonna pick it up right now?"

"Why not?" Thus speaking, Delane smiled as he bent down and picked the gun up and dusted it off, then leaned it against the wall next to the mouth of the cave.

"Hell," ol Chess said, grinning wryly, "I wuz expectin something drastic to happen. Now it makes me wonder just what them Navvies wuz afraid of 'cause they wouldn't even come near it, let alone touch it."

"Well, now, Chess," Delane said with a broad smile, "I touched it and nothing happened, so it's up to you to step inside the cave!"

"Nah, you've got more pull with the Divine Powers than I have! I believe you'd better step inside first."

"For some reason or another, Chess, you seem mighty willing to sacrifice me today!" Delane said laughing. "But I'll go ahead. I'm not the least bit superstitious." So he peered into the cave for a moment, then stepped inside. Nothing happened.

"Well, by thee wars," Chess said grinning broadly, "since you haven't been swallowed up in the bowels of the earth, I believe I **will** come in and join you." Cautiously he stepped up to the entrance, peered in, and seemed to hesitate momentarily.

"C'mon. Git in here!" Delane said with a chuckle. "Nothing's gonna git ya. You can see that nothin's happened to me."

So Chess stepped in and leaned his shovel against the wall. Studying the interior of the cave momentarily, he said, "It feels a little odd in here, Delane. Do you hear a kind of light humming noise?"

"No, I don't hear a thing, but I'd swear there's some heat comin up outa the floor right here. Step over here and feel this sand."

Putting a hand down on the sand, ol Chess looked up, eyes big as saucers. "By golly, there's no doubt about it; this sand's warm, uncommonly warm, and there's no way the sun's rays could git in here. Let's feel this sand here by the opposite wall."

That sand was cool. Then they both felt the warm sand again. "Well, now," Delane said, looking puzzled, "I don't quite know what to say about this. Heat's definitely comin up outa this sand right here."

"I'm wonderin," Chess said while stepping toward the entrance,"if we oughta git the hell outa this joint while the gittin's good."

"No, now let's not git overly excited. Maybe there's a natural explanation for this. Let's think about it a minute."

"There's a natural explanation for it all right," Chess said. "I think someone's sendin us a message tellin us we're where we shouldn't be."

"Do you still hear that humming?"

"I sure'n heck do. In fact, it's a bit louder'n it wuz at first. You can't hear it at all?"

"Can't hear a thing, and I have good ears."

"Well, by thee wars, Delane, I can hear it; and I'm beginnin to feel funny all over."

"Now, we need to talk this over a minute or two. It could be that these signals we've been gittin are positive signals tellin us that we've come to the right place. If some of the stories we've heard about what happened to them Navvies is true, then it musta meant that at that particular time it wasn't intended for the gold statue to be removed, if in fact it actually was a gold statue. Could be that now **is** the time to move it."

"Ja, but not for what we have in mind to do with it! I know what you're a sayin," Chess conceded, feeling an adrenaline rush. "You could be right, and at the same time you might be wrong. I'm beginnin to wonder if we oughta pack up and git outa here.""

"Well, there's one sure way to find out," Delane said, assuming an air of confidence in this ticklish situation. "Let's start diggin, and if we git a specific manifestation of some kind or another that we shouldn't proceed, then we'll replace the sand

and head for home. But one thing about it, the more we delay, the more we're runnin the risk of them fellers comin up here and ketchin us diggin. Then the fat's in the fire. They're not gonna believe that your Navajo grandmother buried her purse in this sand!"

Though looking confused and doubtful, ol Chess finally gave in. "Okay, then, let's start diggin. But we'd better be on the lookout for any strange signs. This hummin sound's still pretty loud, and it don't act to me like it wants to stop either."

Taking the initiative, Delane pressed his shovel into the warm sand and tossed the first shovelful to the other side of the cave. Then he proceeded to shovel steadily for about ten minutes. Every little while Chess stepped to the mouth of the cave to survey their immediate surroundings to see if they had company. "Delane," he said finally, "d'ya think I oughta slip down there to the pickup and git them rifles?"

"Might not be a bad idea." Visibly relieved to get out of the cave and away from that confounded humming, Chess went down to fetch the rifles while the digging proceeded. When Delane paused for a moment to pick up a handful of sand, he noticed with alarm that it was even warmer than that on the surface. Just then Chess returned with their rifles.

"This sand now's even warmer," Delane said, forcing himself to grin. "Come and feel it for yourself. Wuz ya ever in a situation quite like this before?"

"Frankly no," came the response. "I've been in some tight pinches but never one quite like this."

"Well, we'll keep diggin for a while, Chess. There must be something down here because this sand keeps gittin warmer the deeper I go. By the way, d'ya wanna trade me off for a minute or two? I need to step outside and git a breath o' fresh air myself."

So Chess, hesitantly at first, took over the digging. Every few shovelfuls he'd test the temperature of the sand. Soon the sweat was pouring off his brow but not just from the physical exertion of shoveling; he was beginning to feel an even greater emotional strain, something wholly new to him, for he'd always been a happy-go-lucky sort and didn't normally let anything bother him.

Observing him for a moment or two, Delane said, "What d'ya think? Is the sand gittin gradually warmer?"

"Yes, 'fraid so."

"What 'll we do if it gits so warm we can't stand bein in the cave?"

"Well, sir, I don't rightly know. But I guess if the soles of our boots git to smokin, that might be the signal for making tracks outa here. . . ."

"You'd better go and take a little breather, Chess. Meantime, I'll git on the upper end of that ignorant stick and see how much sand I can move."

Finally down to a depth of four feet with half of the sand piled upon the other half of the space in the cave, both men noted that each shovelful seemed to be a bit hotter than the one before it. But being so close to "pay dirt," Delane doggedly kept diggin for another twelve or sixteen inches, when suddenly he noticed emanating from a portion of the lower wall what appeared to be a slight bit of smoke or steam, some kind of an odorless exhalation.

"Hell, Delane," Chess said, his tones belying alarm, "if there's explosives buried down in here and this whole sombitch blows up, folks 'll be pickin up pieces of us off the sage and cedars for a half mile around! D'ya think we oughta quit this place while we can?"

"I've thought about it, thought seriously about it. But, Chess, it's like this. For someone to have buried explosives in here would be the sickest joke I've heard about in recent years. And if after all this work we pick up an leave, some of those other yahoos are gonna come here and reap the fruits of all our labors. Now, I don't know if it's intuition or stupidity, hopefully not the latter, but whatever it is, I'm willin to risk it. I think we're on to something, something big. Within a mere matter of minutes, you and I could be potentially RICH men!"

"Well, jus keep diggin away," Chess said, forcing a smile. "I'll stand just outside o' the entrance and off to the side with my fingers in both ears just in case this place goes up like one big whoop in hell!"

153

"Well, it's like this," Delane said with a chuckle. "If that should happen, neither one of us would hear or feel a thing. As for your standin outside, that might be better anyway right at the moment. You'll be able to keep an eye out for uninvited company." Then gently applying the tip of his shovel blade to the spot where fumes of some kind were escaping, he removed some of the sand. Like a bloodhound that's picked up the scent, he took a fairly large shovelful out of the place and noticed that the sand from this wall area was bordering on what could be called hot. Suddenly his shovel struck something solid, but it didn't feel or sound like a rock. "Chess!" he called out. "Git in here quick! I think I've found something!"

Stepping inside with a look of apprehension as if the place might be ready to go sky high, Chess said timidly, "What is it anyway?"

"There's something solid, but it don't feel like a rock or anything like that. If I'm not mistaken, it feels somewhat like wood."

"Wood! What in hell 'd wood be doin down in there?"

"I don't know, but that's what it feels like." Delane then continued to remove sand from the recessed area till he could see a portion of a manmade object. "We **got** something here, Chess!" he said excitedly and continued digging. "Yes, there's no doubt about it! We got something here! But it's too big for me to manage alone. Hop down in here and help me move this thing. It looks like a wooden crate of some kind."

Ol Chess' emotions now a combination of excitement and reluctance, he carefully slid down into the excavated area and took a look. "By thee wars, Delane," he exclaimed almost ecstatically, "you're **right**! Why, I can **see** it! It **is** a crate. Why, I've never been so excited since the last time I caught my pants on fire! But hell, man, I hope this thing doesn't turn out to be an Egyptian mummy!"

Smiling, Delane said, "No chance o' that. I can tell from the way the crate reacts to our pulling and prying that it can't be more'n about two feet long and about that wide."

After pulling and prying some more, they dug out more sand from around the object, and again pulling and prying they were able to make a slight bit of headway, pulling the crate an inch or so toward them.

"Wait just a minute," Delane said. "Let me dig some of the dirt away from the face of the wall so we can git a better hold on this thing."

Presently they could see the crate clearly. "Are we awake or dreaming?" Chess said. "Hell, I'm expectin to wake up any minute now and hear the wife tell me to stop twistin and squirmin and snortin around!"

"Here, Chess," Delane said, "see if you can reach back in there to git hold of the far end of the thing, and I'll do the same on this side. There, you got hold of it? Ja? Now, on the count o' three, pull like heck. One, two, **three!**"

The effort paid off, for they pulled the crate a good six inches further outa the niche. Looking at one another and grinning, each one perceiving dollar signs in the other's eyes, they kept inching the crate out of the hole until it was all the way out. "I can't believe this, Chess," Delane said, his voice breaking with emotion. "Here, let's take one of these slats off and see if we can remove this side panel enough to see inside."

With the panel opened up, they saw what appeared to be clay or something similar.

"D'ya know what, Chess? Whatever's inside this crate is packed in clay for protection."

"Yes, I can see it myself!" Chess said, face flushed with anticipation. "Now gently chip away some of the clay right here on the edge so we can see what's in there. Put one of the larger pieces in your pocket so we can analyze it out in the better light."

"I hope this thing don't contain explosives!" Delane said.

"Hell, perish the thought. This thing blows up, and you'll be **Admiral** Perish!"

"Admiral Perish, huh!" Delane said laughing. "Anyway, here goes." Applying the shovel blade to the corner of the exposed area inside the crate, he tapped gently with no results. So tapping a little harder, he finally succeeded in breaking off a piece. "I'm gonna keep this for a souvenir."

"Keep goin," Chess said to encourage him. "By gum, we're onto something here."

Tapping even harder, Delane finally knocked off a good section of clay, this time exposing a bright yellow metal. Swallowing hard but not taking his eyes off the exposed area, he said, "My friend, do you SEE WHAT I SEE! THERE'S GOLD INSIDE THIS CRATE!!"

Ol Chess let out a war whoop that could 've been heard a block or two away! "Hell, Ruth," he exclaimed, "don't wake me up now! This is one dream I've gotta see to the finish!"

Laughing with boyish excitement, Delane said, "Quick, Chess! Let's lift this thing up outa here and git it down to the pickup and head for the wickiup!"

After a bit of straining and groaning and grunting, they managed to lift the crate up out of the hole; then with great care they carried it down the embankment and down to the pickup.

"Chess," Delane said, "spread one of these bedrolls over the crate so nobody 'll git suspicious if he sees it. Meantime, I'll go back up there to git the shovels and the guns, including that old rusted-out Navajo rifle."

Soon back with those items, Delane said, "I wish to heck I'd a thought to bring my lasso along so we could have tied this crate down in the back of the pickup and stabilized it. As it is, by the time we git to town, no tellin what shape the crate 'll be in. Might have to have you sit back here, Chess, and keep the thing from slidin around or even bouncin out."

"Well, for now let's git outa here while the gittin's good!" Chess said. "I'll keep a close eye on the crate."

"Oh, no, don't tell me!" Delane exclaimed, pointing off in the distance. "Look who's comin!"

"By thee wars, wouldn't you know it!" Chess said. "That's them big Texans. They're followin our tire tracks."

"And there's no place to hide," Delane said resignedly. "Better have a good story ready, Chess, for there's no way we can avoid meetin these guys."

Headin back down to the main drag, they were face to face with the Texans, who appeared to be in a high dudgeon. Putting on a friendly face, Delane said, "How'd do, gentlemen."

"How'd do," the driver replied without smiling. "You fellers told us those caves were down past the oil wells."

"You mean you didn't find 'em?" Delane asked innocently.

"Hell, no, we didn't find 'em! And when we asked those fellers at that first well where the caves were, they acted like we were crazy. 'There's no caves out here that we know of,' one of 'em said laughing, 'but you'll find some down on Grand Bench.' Now that's why we've come back down here, and then we saw your tire tracks headin up through these junipers. How the hell long have you guys been living around here that you wouldn't a known better'n to send us clear down there to hell and gone? Or were you just bullshittin us to git rid of us?"

"No," Chess said, "it wasn't that at all. As for how long we've been living in this area, my partner here has lived around this neck of the woods all his life. Myself," he continued, eyes twinkling, "the first time I come to Escalante, I wuz ridin a mountain lion while holdin a bobcat under each arm and usin a rattlesnake for a quirt, and some mean sombitch run me outa town!"

The outrageousness of ol Chess' story finally broke the tension, causing the Texans to laugh. Then leaning a little closer toward them, he said, "Fellers, let me tell you something. Them fellers over there at the wells aren't from around here. Nary a one of 'em growed up in this this part o' the country and could be expected to know the ins and outs of this vast area. If me and my partner here had the time, we'd take y'all over there and show them caves to you. But we've got to hightail it outa here and be in Panguitch by 8:30 this evenin; otherwise we'd be more'n happy to show you."

"How come you fellers are both all dirty and sweaty? Was it that hard to find the Navajo purse! You haven't been diggin, have you?"

"No," Chess said, "no diggin. Heaven forbid! We shot us a little two-point buck back there and wuz carryin him over an embankment and lost our footing. I believe he rolled over both of us 'fore we got to the bottom. It musta been a comical sight. In fact, I'd a much preferred to a been watchin than participatin in this little incident. We got the carcass covered up with a bedroll to keep the flies off him. There's quite a few deer up in there

157

where you fellers are headed, so if you have your rifles along, you might take a potshot or two at some of 'em."

"Well, we got plenty o' firepower along," the fellow sitting in the middle said. "Ja," the driver added, "since we're gonna be here a day or two, we might just take you at your word and shoot us a buckskin and have a little feast tonight!"

"Not a thing in the world wrong with that," Delane observed. Then after a slight pause he added, "I'm afraid we'd better be hitten the road. Good luck to you fellers. We've gotta fly low if we make it to Panguitch on time. . . ."

Moving again, they greeted the second pickup of Texans in passing. The driver called out, "Say, did you find your grandma's purse?!"

"Right where she left it," Chess called out grinning.

"Whew!" Delane said as they got past them and on their way again. "Another close one."

"Too close for comfort," Chess said. "Now, I'll bet them fellers follow our tracks right up there to the cave and see where we've been diggin, and then they're bound to light in after us. 'Firepower we got,' that one said. And to top it all off, these old big black clouds look heavy with rain, and that means flash floods up ahead."

"I hate to admit it," Delane said, "but I'm afraid you're right. I might have to put my foot in the carburetor and git this old bucket o' bolts a bellerin and squealin. We've gotta put some distance between us and them. Now wouldn't you believe it! See that dust approachin?"

"Ja, I see it, damn it all to hell. That has to be them two Californians."

Minutes later they met. "You fellers lookin for the Texans?" Delane asked.

"Well, not necessarily," the driver said. "I think you gentlemen sent us on a wild goose chase."

"How's that?" Delane asked innocently.

"Well, we got over there by those oil wells, but try as we would, we couldn't find any caves. One of the men said he'd heard the caves were down on Grand Bench. He even said the Navajos had a sacred cave of some kind down there and were afraid to go in it. Do you know anything about it? As speleologists, we're especially interested in looking into a cave like that."

"Yes, we've heard a rumor or two about such a cave," Chess said, "but I've been so busy tendin to my cattle that I've never really took the time to go and investigate it. I suppose I ought to do it one o' these days. Maybe I can even talk my partner here into to comin with me."

"By the way, sir," the Californian said, "were you successful in locating your grandmother's leather bag?"

"Oh, yes," Chess said chuckling. "It wuz right where she said she'd left it."

"You wouldn't mind showing it to us, would you? We've always been interested in native American artifacts."

"Well, I'll tell you," Chess replied, "we'd be more'n happy to dig it out of my bedroll, where I put it for safe keeping on our way home. But these old big black clouds are beginnin to look more and more ominous, and we've got to be in Panguitch this evenin by 8:30 to meet a man leavin for Denver on the Trailways bus. Otherwise we'd be happy to show you. It's just a sheepskin bag 'bout this big and has a drawstring, which is also made of sheep hide. It's good leathercraft though. I wish we had more time. Now good luck to you fellers!"

On their way again, Chess said, "Better kick this old lizzy in the ass, Delane! I have a sneakin suspicion that them three big Texans are gonna be right on our tail 'fore we git outa this place."

The sky now almost completely overcast, they were really worried when the first raindrops started hitting the windshield, each drop plowing a little furrow of sorts as it parted the dust on the glass. "You good at prayin, Chess?" Delane said chuckling. "If you've got any pull with the Man Upstairs, you'd better start petitioning Him to hold this rain back. We've got several bad crossings up ahead as you well know."

"That we do, and there's a number of steep clay dugways to git up over."

"I'd like to push this old Ford a little harder, but I'm afraid if I do, it'll quit on us entirely, and then we'll be between the proverbial rock and a hard place."

"Well, we're making pretty good time, Delane. If the road down through Colletts wasn't rougher'n a cob, I suggest we go that way to throw them fellers off our tracks. But tryin to hurry down through there 'd shake this vehicle all to hell."

"Since they're not too familiar with this area, Chess, they might think we turned south up there by Big Sage and headed down toward Page. Anyway, we'll continue to maintain this steady pace. I've been watchin the heat gauge, and if I try to push ol Charlie's Prodigy here, the thing's gonna vapor lock on us. So you see I can go only so fast. But we're puttin some miles behind us."

"Quite true," Chess agreed, "but you noticed, didn't you, that them Texans, both sets of 'em, had 4-wheel-drive pickups?"

"Yes, I noticed, and I'm concerned about it."

By now the rain was coming down harder with each flash of lightning and peal of thunder. And the situation was really compounded when in the rearview mirror Delane noticed that they were being pursued. "Well, Chess, better put your flak jacket on 'cause we've got unwanted company, and they seem to be in a hurry. You see, they've gone up to that cave and climbed down into the hole and noticed the recessed area back in the wall and the markings in the sand left by the crate when we pulled it out. Why in the dickens did it not occur to us to cover that little niche up?"

"There's your 20/20 hindsight jus kickin in, Delane!" Chess commented. "We wuz in such a rip-snortin hurry to git outa there that safety measures of any kind failed to cross our gourds. And look how much blacker them clouds are up ahead. What in the sam hell 're we gonna do if we encounter some flash floods comin down through some of them big washes?"

"Well, if by the time we git there and the water's not too deep, we probably can git across. I might have to git a little run on it. Course, now, we'll have to size things up pretty good. I don't want to pull a Berlin Osborn and git out there'n the middle of one of them washes and have the flood come right up over the

160

hood of the pickup like it did him that time he tried to cross the wash there south of town. Me and Uncle Joe Schow and Burnard had to go out there with Uncle Joe's team when the water had subsided a bit and pull him out. All three of us wuz covered with mud from one end to the other, and ol Berlin looked like a thrice-drowned gopher!"

"By thee wars, Delane, them fellers is a gainin on us fast."

"Yes, I see they are. They're a blinkin their headlights for us to stop, but we can't risk it. They've put two and two together and decided that it's no deer we have under this bedroll."

"What're we gonna do?" Chess asked in alarm.

"Well, the only thing I can see to do at the moment is to keep goin and hope them buzzards back there slide off the road or something. But they're not lettin up, and the lead vehicle keeps blinkin its headlights."

"Hell, Delane," Chess exclaimed while looking back, "them fellers can't be more a block behind us right now."

Moments later a shot rang out as a slug came crashing right between Delane and Chess and out the windshield. "Great Ned!" Chess hollered. "Now that's gittin way too close for comfort. Them bastards back there must be maniacs to pull a stunt like that."

"I think they musta been aimin for one of our tires," Delane said with alarm. "And these dadblasted wipers won't move fast enough to keep the rain off. We've practically got a cloudburst here now."

"Oh, joy!" Chess called out. "Look what's up ahead. That's that bad wash. D'ya think we can make it across?"

"I believe we can," Delane said. "The water don't appear to be too deep. I'll floorboard this old lizzy and see if we can bull our way through to the other side!"

But at the very moment they started their rapid descent into the wash, a mammoth wall of flood water crashed into them, rolling the pickup over several times and carrying them about thirty-five yards downstream, where the old Ford landed upright as it lodged against a big rock. The cab was filled with muddy water up to the windows, the glass of which had either been broken or shaken out, which was a blessing since at least half of

161

the water immediately drained out of the cab. In all o' the rumbling and tumbling the two men had changed places, and ol Chess' head was down between the brake and the clutch. Rousing enough to apprehend the situation, Delane pulled with all the strength he could muster and finally got Chess' head up outa the water. The old feller looked like a gonner there for a minute, but Delane shook him and pounded on his back to git him coughing up muddy water until he finally started to catch his breath.

Looking like a big mud-covered rat that had been pulled through a knot hole, ol Chess, after getting stabilized somewhat, said between spurts of coughing and gagging, "My word, Delane, now I can say I've been to hell and back!"

"That makes two of us!" Delane said. "Tell me, Chess. Do I look as bad as you do?!"

"Great Caesar's balls, I wouldn't even know ya if I met ya on the street. All I can see of you is eyes and teeth. The rest of you's caked with mud." This said, Chess got on another coughing and gagging spree, an amazing volume of muddy water coming out of his mouth. "Hell," he said finally, "I've got so damned much top soil inside me that a man could plant crops all through my gut!"

Despite their desperate situation, Delane had to laugh. "Chess," he said, still laughing, "humor's your salvation. I believe you'd crack jokes goin over Niagara Falls!"

"Well, I'll tell you," Chess said between spells of coughing and gagging and spitting up mud, "it's a damn sight better to laugh than it is to cry. I know this well 'cause I've tried both, and years ago I decided to hell with that cryin business. I'll laugh from now on if it kills me!"

"Oh, my Lard!" Delane said, suddenly sounding sober. "Wonder if that crate o' gold's still in the back of the pickup!" Though the flood waters were still raging, he managed to pull himself halfway out of the passenger-side window to have a look. His heart sank. "Chess," he said, his voice registering despair, "it's gone! There's not a trace of it or of anything else in the back of the pickup! Only God Himself can know where it is now."

162

If Chess hadn't had so much mud on his face, one could have seen how white he'd turned. "Delane," he said, no humor in his voice this time, "I'm heart sick. Hell, we had us a million bucks in the back o' this pickup, and now it's gone. . . . Ruth, you can wake me up any time now. I believe I've had enough of this hellish dream."

But Ruth, unfortunately, didn't wake him up. There he and Delane sat looking like two mud-covered rats to face the very ugly music. Both men, ineffably disappointed, sat there for a moment, heads bowed as if in prayer but neither one praying. Both of them were thinking about what might have been **and** should have been.

"Hell, Delane," Chess said, his voice breaking, "we had it right in our very hands. Why didn't we think about hidin it out there somewhere and then come back to git it when the coast was clear?"

"There's some 20/20 hindsight," Delane said philosophically.

"Well," Chess said, "I've picked in the horse manure with the chickens all my life, so I guess this means goin right back to the barnyard and pickin up where I left off."

"Well, now, my friend," Delane said after a moment's reflection, "we've got to look at the positive side of things. We could a been drowned, you know; and maybe we should a been, but I'm sure glad we weren't! I feel somewhat like the old Southern preacher who said, 'I's not much, but I's all I got!' And, aside from losin all that gold, both of us can say that we've come away with something of infinitely greater value---our very lives."

"Yes, you're right," Chess said reflectively. "I guess that Feller up Above musta been lookin out for us after all. I've got to remember to look up and say a big Thank You before hittin the sack tonight. . . ."

EPILOGUE

Time, inexorable time, is impervious to all human attempts at intervention. For time proceeds unabated, irrespective of the wishes of humankind. Time may bring joy or grief or shame or disappointment and an infinite number of additional qualities and non-qualities. And in the course of time, time can change human perspectives as much as 180 degrees. Often in course of time a Higher Power intercedes as in the case of El Nino. This 50-pound block of gold was temporarily in the hands of two mortals who had vague notions of using it as a means of self-aggrandizement, the eyes of each one's imagination revealing a wide variety of things and activities to bring pleasure and otherwise to titillate the senses. But in fairness to them, it must be said that they conceived these various notions in total ignorance, for neither of them had any inkling of the significance, indeed the supernal purposes, of El Nino. In fine, neither of them knew for sure what was inside that crate except that they had seen what appeared to be gold. What would have been their reactions if they had known beforehand the significance of El Nino and had known that El Nino was actually in their possession? Moot questions indeed! All they knew for sure was that an "earthly" heaven appeared to be in their grasp; but as things turned out, their treasure proved to be much too slippery for them, much as in ancient times when men whose hearts were on their treasures thought to bury them in the ground for safekeeping, only to return and find them gone. But such slippery treasures had not been removed by human hands. . . .

Well, the Texans, also blinded by the huge $ signs in their eyes, were filled with both chagrin for their deplorable actions and with compassion for the plight of the two Escalante men whom they had pursued unmercifully. Despite the unabating downpour, they got out of their pickups and carefully made their way down along the east bank of the flood-filled wash to a spot directly opposite from the stranded men, realizing all the while that the treasure they had intended to gain control of was no longer in their possession. Calling out to them, they said, "Hang on, fellers! Just as soon as these flood waters subside, we'll come down and rescue you."

They intended to keep their word; but as things turned out, Chess and Delane, waiting until it was safe, climbed out of the poor old smashed-up pickup and onto the huge rock against which it had lodged and then slid down onto solid ground. Minutes later they had made their way back up to the road. By this time the rain had lessened to a mere sprinkle and a great calm had settled over the area. The Texans then drove across the wash and, now in possession of their normal sense and good judgment, apologized to the stranded men, both of whom they drove home to Escalante. No charges were filed against the one Texan for attempted murder and against the others for being accessories to the attempted crime. Not surprisingly, these men left for Texas within minutes of dropping off the two victims and have never been seen in or around Escalante since then.

Subsequently, Chess and Delane returned again and again to that ill-fated wash just west of Grand Bench but were never successful in finding so much as a trace of their crate of gold. Others, too, spent many days searching in vain. Successive floods finally swept the old Ford farther downstream and eventually buried it, thus obliterating all traces of the supposed treasure.

Over the years the two Escalante cowpokes were kept busy telling, retelling, and embellishing their story of "almost." Some believed them; others doubted, making them feel at times like the guy who told of the big fish that got away. If people caught Delane in the right mood, he'd even show them that piece of clay that he had chipped from the outside of El Nino. He still has it to this day, but I can't vouch for his present willingness to show it to anyone. As for Chess, well, he's riding that silver saddle up there in those unending meadows in the sky, his riches now far greater than any that the melting-down of El Nino could have provided.

The Navajos eventually discovered that the treasure in their erstwhile unapproachable cave, whatever kind of treasure it might have been, had been removed and that they now could enter the cave with impunity. And yet, in time, they came to regard the cave as sacred. Some of them even insisted that many of their sick had been healed by visiting the cave, which gradually came to be looked upon as a shrine and still is to this day.

As for El Nino, well, he of course is the undisputed hero of this tale. His powers cannot be fathomed, certainly not by anyone in this world. You're wondering, naturally, what ever happened to this exquisitely crafted gold statue with the incredibly lifelike eyes, which to look upon brought healing to those who had faith---and condemnation to those who came harboring ulterior motives of self-aggrandizement. Famed Padre Silvaro de Escalante, suave, handsome, sophisticated, streaks of silver now gracing his hair, likewise wondered about El Nino and about the propriety of recovering the sacred statue, for the revolutionary spirit in Northern Mexico had subsided for the time being. At least one of the three faithful souls (very likely Sanchez) whom he had commissioned to hide the precious statue in the sacred cave up on Grand Bench would have to be recommissioned to recover it so that once again it could assume its rightful place in the Cathedral of the Blessed Virgin.

But these worries proved to be self-negating when early one morning the padre entered the cathedral for his own private devotions before the parishioners and others began arriving for the first services. Having let himself in through a side door, he followed his usual custom of walking leisurely down to the far end of the chapel, from where, after pausing briefly to survey the whole interior of that beautiful edifice, he'd cross himself while gazing upon the replica of the crucified and suffering Christ at the front end of the chapel. Then he'd walk slowly, eyes trained on the object of his devotion, until standing directly in front of the same he'd cross himself again before kneeling and praying that his thoughts might be garnished with wisdom and inspiration for the day's activities.

On the morning in question, however, when he paused to look at the replica of the crucified Savior, his gaze was diverted immediately to something that utterly took his breath away. For there, mounted naturally in its wonted place, was the statue of El Nino, more radiant than ever and looking as if it had always been

167

there! Gulping hard and feeling his knees sagging, he reflexively put a hand on the nearest pew to steady himself as he went down. Blinking several times to make sure his eyes weren't playing tricks on him, he remained on his knees for the next several minutes, his natural strength having drained out of him. Once he was able to stand up again, he walked slowly and carefully toward the front of the chapel, eyes all the while glued immovably on the statue of El Nino to make sure the transcendent "vision" didn't dematerialize. There he prostrated himself before this Commanding Presence. Finally arising, he gazed steadfastly into the eyes of El Nino, a great surge of power suddenly coursing through his body from the roots of his hair to the tips of his toes. "**El Nino, you're back!**" he whispered. Then, tears coursing down his face, he exclaimed with gusto, "**<u>El Nino, you're back</u>!**"

Wholly incapable of formulating a rational explanation for this phenomenon, the padre suddenly perceived the words of Isaiah coming into his mind: **"For my thoughts are not your thoughts, neither are your ways my ways, saith the LORD. For as the heavens are higher than the earth, so are my ways higher than your ways, and my thoughts than your thoughts . . . ."**

The End

About the Author

Ferrel Glade Roundy has been an English professor for over thirty years. Upon retiring from the teaching profession, he will return with his wife to their native southern Utah and their 160 acres of sage and cedars to build a home and to bask in the inimitable beauty in and around the Grand Staircase-Escalante National Monument. In that pristine environment Ferrel will continue to write, adding to the dozen or so books he already has authored.

Check the 1stBooks website for other books by Ferrel Glade Roundy:

TRAGEDY AND TRIUMPH IN SCHWEINFURT—Memoirs of a Jewish Pig Farmer in the Third Reich

UP FROM THE ASHES—The Story of Jim, Miss Watson's Former Slave

FAMED STORYTELLER CHESS LAY TELLS TALL TALES OF ESCALANTE

BEYOND THE ROAD TO DAMASCUS—Saul of Tarsus Becomes Paul the Apostle

HUCK FINN GOES WEST—The Continuing Story of this Legendary Hero